CHARMED

To Michele, the newest Aronson sister—and to Bill too

Thanks for their sage advice to:
Steve Aronson
Kathleen Cotter
Ellen Loughran
Joe Morton
and especially my editor, Jon Lanman

CHARMED

MARILYN SINGER

ATHENEUM 1990 NEW YORK

Collier Macmillan Canada
Toronto

Maxwell Macmillan International Publishing Group
New York Oxford Singapore Sydney

Atheneum
Macmillan Publishing Company
866 Third Avenue
New York, NY 10022

Collier Macmillan Canada, Inc.
1200 Eglinton Avenue East
Suite 200
Don Mills, Ontario M3C 3N1

First edition
Designed by Nancy B. Williams
Printed in the United States of America
1 2 3 4 5 6 7 8 9 10

Singer, Marilyn.
Charmed/by Marilyn Singer.—1st ed.
p. cm.
Summary: Twelve-year-old Miranda and her companion Bastable, an invisible catlike
creature from another world, discover that they are part of the Correct Combination,
a team that must stop the evil Charmer from taking over the universe.
ISBN 0–689–31619–4
[1. Fantasy.] I. Title.
PZ7.S6172Ch 1990
[Fic]—dc20   90-518
CIP
AC

CHAPTER

I

Miranda yawned. It was a real window-rattler of a yawn. She called it the Tired Lion, and she was rather proud of it. Miranda had a repertoire of other yawns as well—the Exhausted Elephant, the Disinterested Dog, the Bored Water Buffalo, among them—but the Tired Lion was her personal favorite.

Miranda's father pretended not to hear it. Her mother frowned, but didn't say a word. As for Uncle Gerald, he was too involved in showing the slides of his latest trip to notice. Twice a year he came to Miranda's house to show slides, and, as far as Miranda was concerned, that was twice a year too often. It was a mystery to her how a person could make the most fascinating places in the world seem dull, but Uncle Gerald had a real knack for it.

"This is the Sheesh Mahal or Palace of Mirrors. It was built by a maharajah—which, as you know, is the Indian equivalent of a king—for his maharanee—or queen. Construction commenced in 1657 and was completed in 1668," Uncle Gerald was droning now.

Miranda let out another yawn, a smaller one this time, sort of a Drowsy Dormouse, and looked at the slide of the lovely palace, its pink marble towers glowing against a bright blue sky. Shutting out the sound of her uncle's voice, she began to imagine what it would be like to live there. She was good at imagining. She could see herself dressed in a purple-and-silver sari, riding an elephant among the cypress trees in the large and elegant garden. Someone was coming to meet her. It was one of her councillors, no doubt seeking her advice on how to avoid war with the neighboring maharajah or on some other important issue. With long-legged strides, he approached her and bowed until she gave him permission to speak. But before she could grant it a familiar voice whispered in her ear, "He calls that pitiful domicile a palace? In Appledura our peasants wouldn't live in such a place."

"Bastable!" Miranda shrieked and nearly fell off the couch. Immediately she became aware of a shocked and puzzled silence in the room. She turned her head. Uncle Gerald and her parents were staring at her. *Whoops*, she thought.

"Miranda, my dear, are you all right?" Uncle Gerald asked.

"Me?" Miranda said innocently. "Why, yes. I'm fine. In fact, I couldn't be better."

"She must have been daydreaming again. She's a great one for daydreaming," said her mother. "Aren't you, Miranda?"

"Excuse me, please. I need to go to the bathroom," was Miranda's reply.

When she got there, she shut the door with a bang, whirled around, and exploded, "Bastable, how many times have I told you never to sneak up on me like that?"

"I did not sneak up on you. You were simply not paying attention," sniffed the creature standing before her. He looked a lot like a rather large cat. But he could walk on two legs as well as four, use his front paws like clawed hands, and he was completely invisible—except when he chose not to be or when he was unconscious—to any human but Miranda. "Furthermore," he continued haughtily, "in Appledura, we, the King of the Fenines, never wait for an audience. The audience waits for us."

"Appledura, Appledura, Appledura! I'm sick to death of hearing about Appledura," Miranda said peevishly. "You're not in Appledura anymore. You're stuck here just like me in good old Bassberg—where, as you found out, there aren't even any bass—probably for the rest of our lives." As soon as the words were out, Miranda wished she could take them back.

Bastable's tail drooped. His fine fur sagged. His eyes lost their proud gleam. "Alas, I fear you're quite right," he said miserably, sitting down on the floor.

Contritely, Miranda plunked herself beside him. "Oh, Bastable, don't mind me. I'm just grumpy today. You'll get back to Appledura. I know you will." She reached out to stroke him, but withdrew her hand. It didn't seem appropriate to pet a king—even if he did resemble a tabby cat.

Bastable didn't respond to either her gesture or words. He knew even better than Miranda did that there was little hope. It was six long months ago, Earth time, that he'd been forced to give up his kingship, his homeland, even his world, and arrive on this poor excuse for a planet. If he hadn't somehow found Miranda (she would, of course, claim she'd found him), he would be, at present, in far worse straits. Miranda was, for all her faults, generally good company, Bastable thought. He might have even called her a friend—if kings were allowed to call anyone such a thing.

They both sat there in moody silence until Miranda's mother knocked on the door. "Are you all right in there?" she asked.

"I'm fine," Miranda answered.

"Well, you're taking an awfully long time," she said, lowering her voice to a hoarse whisper. "Stop being rude to your uncle, Miranda. He has a gift he wants to give you."

Miranda's ears perked up. A gift? Uncle Gerald had never bought her a gift before. Uncle Gerald only bought pretty things for himself, which he talked about in great detail whenever they visited his house.

"We'll . . . I mean *I'll* be right out," Miranda called. Then she said in a low voice, "Come on, Bastable. Let's go see what Uncle Gerald's gift is."

"Gifts." Bastable sighed. "I could tell you stories of the gifts I've received. A brush and comb of solid gold. A breastplate worked in pearls. A jeroboam of tuna fish wine."

"Tuna fish wine? Ugh." Miranda grimaced.

The fenine king drew himself up and gave her an imperious look. "You humans have no appreciation for the finer things of life." He stood up, smoothed down his fur, and began to walk through the bathroom wall out toward the street.

"Where are you going?" Miranda asked.

"Out," was all he said. And then he was gone.

Miranda shrugged. "He'll be back," she said, more flippantly than she felt, for she knew if Bastable did leave for good she'd miss him very much indeed. Then she rose and went to the den.

"Ah, here she is," Uncle Gerald greeted her. "Tummy feeling better?"

Miranda gave him a blank look.

"Much better, right, Miranda?" said her mother, smiling at her too broadly.

Miranda ignored her. "Can I have my present now?" she said.

"Miranda!" her father warned sharply, the first thing he'd said to her all night.

But Uncle Gerald chuckled. "It's quite all right, Henry. If I were Miranda, I would be quite eager to receive this gift as well." He bent down behind the screen, lifted up a bulky round thing wrapped in brown paper, and handed it to her.

What could it be, she wondered, balancing the awkward but light shape. She'd been hoping for a sari or some dangling earrings, but this package was certainly neither. Still, it could be something even more special. Uncle Gerald certainly seemed to think it was. "Go ahead, Miranda. Open it," he said excitedly. Without further delay, she ripped off the paper.

There in front of her was a basket. A very old, very plain basket, short and squat, with a few nondescript and faded designs painted here and there on the sides and lid.

"Look at that, Miranda. Isn't it lovely?" her mother exclaimed.

Miranda didn't reply. She didn't think the basket was lovely at all. She thought it was a big disappointment. Unless perhaps... she stared at the lid... there was something inside.

"It's a genuine Kakalumi snake charmer's basket," said Uncle Gerald. "Two hundred years old. I would have kept it myself, but I simply don't have room for another basket. The Kakalumi developed a most unique weaving technique...."

As Uncle Gerald elaborated on the Kakalumi, Miranda lifted the lid and let it dangle from its cord against the basket's side. She bent her head and peered into it. There was nothing there but a funny smell.

"Fascinating," Miranda's mother said.

"Expensive," mused her father.

"A-choo!" sneezed Miranda, recognizing the smell. Mildew. It always made her sneeze.

"Actually, I got it for practically nothing," said Uncle Gerald. "The man who sold it to me wanted to get rid of it."

"Why should he want to do that?"

"Well, it has a little water damage. But I don't really think that was the reason. He seemed a bit... afraid of it. Though I can't imagine why."

"Really. How interesting," said Miranda's mother. "Don't you think so, Miranda?"

"A-choo!" Miranda replied.

"Oh, dear, are you coming down with a cold? I think you'd better go right to bed."

Without protest, Miranda got up and headed for the door.

"Aren't you going to say good-night to Uncle Gerald first?"

"Good-night, Uncle Gerald."

"And thank him for the present?" said her father, picking up the basket and putting it in Miranda's arms.

"Thanks, Uncle Gerald," Miranda said unenthusiastically.

Uncle Gerald didn't seem to notice. "You're welcome, Miranda. And remember, if you have any questions about the Kakalumi, I can supply you with an excellent reading list."

"I'll remember that, Uncle Gerald," Miranda said.

Bumping her way to her room, Miranda sneezed twice more, banged her elbow on a door jamb, and kicked at the leg of her mother's china cabinet. "Phooey!" she exclaimed, dumping her burden on the floor in the corner of her room. Kakalumi snake basket indeed. What a stupid, boring present. What a stupid, boring night. And now not even Bastable was around to liven things up. "Bastable," she called softly. But the fenine didn't appear.

"Phooey," said Miranda again, and for the third time that evening, she let out a yawn. This one was a perfect imitation of a weary twelve-year-old girl.

"Passion Fruit," Pamela declared.

"Racy Raspberry," suggested Suzanne.

"I like Mango Tango best," Amy Beth argued.

"It doesn't go with your hair," Suzanne said flatly.

"Yes, it does. Redheads can wear orange tones. My mother said so."

"What do you think, Miranda?" Pamela turned and held out Amy Beth's hand on which were three broad smears of lipstick. "Which one would you pick?"

"Dorothy, I guess," Miranda replied.

"Huh?"

"I'd pick Dorothy. Her adventures in Oz were a lot better than Alice's in Wonderland or Wendy's in Never Never Land."

"What's she talking about this time?" Amy Beth clucked.

"I don't know why you bother to ask her anything," Suzanne sneered. "She never listens."

Miranda blushed, but in a loud, unapologetic voice she proclaimed, "I was thinking about something else."

"She always is," said Suzanne.

"What were you thinking about?" Pamela asked curiously.

"I was wondering, if I had the chance, which character I'd prefer to be—Dorothy from *The Wizard of Oz*, Alice from *Alice in Wonderland*, or Wendy in *Peter Pan*."

"Don't you think you're a little old for those stories?"
Amy Beth asked.

"She wants to *be* Peter Pan and never grow up."
Suzanne laughed.

Then Miranda's mother came into her room for a moment. "Your father's here, Amy Beth, to take you girls home."

"Already?" Amy Beth always pretended to be disappointed when she had to leave. Miranda wasn't sure why. Nor was she certain why Amy Beth and the other girls bothered to come over to her house. But she guessed it might have something to do with the fact that Miranda's mother was willing to let them try on her makeup, and also that Miranda, being an only child, had no sisters or brothers around, bratty or otherwise, to spoil their fun. The only party pooper was Miranda herself, who tolerated the girls because her mother was so insistent upon her having some "nice friends" come over. The one girl Miranda had genuinely liked had recently moved away; the one boy, her mother found "odd." She said he reminded her of a cat burglar in a movie she once saw and she didn't particularly want him in her house. *Mom should see Bastable*, Miranda thought, and felt a strand of worry thread through her. Two nights had passed since Uncle Gerald's visit and Bastable hadn't returned. He couldn't still be annoyed with her, could he? Or had he actually found a way to return to Appledura and disappeared without so much as a good-bye?

"Good-bye, Miranda," Amy Beth said.

"See you in school," said Pamela.

"She's not listening again." Suzanne shook her head,

stepped back, and bumped into Uncle Gerald's basket, which was lying near the door. "What's this thing?" she asked.

Miranda looked at it and blinked. *I could swear I put that in the corner*, she thought. "A Kakalumi snake charmer's basket," she answered.

"Ugh, snakes!" exclaimed both Suzanne and Amy Beth.

"Is there a snake in there?" asked Pamela.

"Not now," answered Miranda.

"That's good," said Suzanne. "I wouldn't come here ever again if you had a snake."

"Oh, well. I was thinking of getting one," Miranda said casually.

"Ugh!" chorused Suzanne and Amy Beth, and they hurried out of the room.

Miranda smiled slowly at their retreating backs. Then she realized Pamela was watching her. "You don't like us much, do you?" she said.

"Not much," Miranda replied bluntly.

Pamela responded with a small, rueful chuckle and followed her friends out.

When they'd gone, Miranda's mother returned. "Have a good time?" she asked.

"It was okay."

"They're nice girls." When Miranda didn't say anything, her mother sighed slightly and said, "Your father and I are going out tonight. Should I ask Mrs. Jones to come and stay with you or do you think you can take care of yourself?"

Miranda looked at her mother with surprise and pleasure. She'd never been asked before if she wanted Mrs. Jones. Mrs. Jones was always just there without the asking. "I can take care of myself," Miranda said.

"Good. Your father and I think you can too." Turning to leave, her mother glanced down at the floor. "Oh, by the way, I cleaned out this basket. It was all mildewy."

"Thanks, Mom," Miranda said politely, although she didn't care. *The Mystery of the Moving Basket solved,* she said to herself. When her mother had gone, she once again dumped it unceremoniously in the farthest corner of her room.

"Here's your purse, Mom. And Dad, don't forget your glasses," urged Miranda, handing the things to her parents.

"Can't wait to get rid of us, eh?" said her father good-humoredly.

Although he was exactly right, Miranda didn't tell him so. "I'm just trying to be helpful." She shrugged.

"Now, remember, keep the door locked and don't let anyone in. In case of emergency, you have the phone number of where we'll be. Try not to eat too much junk and get to bed by ten," her mother said, wrapping a fancy shawl around herself.

"Okay, Mom."

A few moments later, Miranda's parents were gone. She felt a heady burst of freedom. *I'm alone,* she thought. *All alone. No Mom and Dad. No Mrs. Jones. I've got the house all to myself and I can do whatever I want to do.* She hugged herself, then wondered, *Okay, so what do I want to do?* Her homework was done, so she turned on the TV and flicked through the channels. But nothing seemed worth watching. *I'd rather read anyway*, she told herself. She picked up *Mary Poppins* from the coffee table and opened it. She'd already read it six times. It was one of her favorite books. But now it seemed a bit silly and childish, and she shut it. *I guess I should try another book*, she thought. But she didn't really feel like reading either. Nor did she want to play solitaire, call anyone on the phone, or clean up her room.

I wonder what I'd be doing right now if I lived somewhere else, she asked herself. It was a game she often played, one that got her accused of daydreaming more times than she cared to count. But there was nobody around to accuse her now. *I wonder what I'd be doing if I lived in* . . . she closed her eyes . . . *Appledura*. Appledura! Her eyes snapped open. *Even when Bastable's not here, that word, that place keeps turning up like a TV commercial I've seen too many times*, Miranda grumbled silently. *Where is he anyway?*

She thought back to when they'd met. It was in Marsh Mallow Park, which, as Uncle Gerald had once explained, was named after a plant and not for the things you toast over campfires, a fact Miranda found rather useless. In the park she'd been practicing bows and curtseys—the kind she'd seen the night before in a movie about Queen Elizabeth I, with a lot of knee-bending and hand flourishes. She was in the middle of a particularly deep dip, her hands outstretched at her sides as though she were holding out her skirts, when Bastable materialized right before her eyes. She promptly plopped down on her rear end.

"You may rise now," he'd told her.

"I may, but I can't," she'd answered when she found her voice. Her legs had jellified and she kept rubbing her eyes to wake herself up.

But eventually she'd realized that she was not dreaming, that Bastable was, in fact, quite real. He told her that he came from a faraway place called Appledura, and that for reasons he did not explain he'd been forced to leave. He'd found his way to Earth via an ancient door between worlds. He had stumbled upon it in his exile and he was not certain he could ever find it again. The door had led straight to Bassberg. For the past week or so since he'd arrived, he'd been fishing in the parks, but he'd only come up with a few bony catfish and no bass. He'd been about to try the pond one more time when he'd noticed Miranda. "I observed you for several minutes," he said. "You are the first human I've seen display a respectful attitude toward royalty. You'll make an acceptable ambassador for me. So I've decided to reveal myself to you—and only to you."

It took Miranda several months to set him straight about her real attitude toward monarchs and the like. By then, she knew that Bastable had not chosen her for her courtliness at all, but because he'd been tired and hungry and very alone, and he'd guessed that Miranda would help him out.

Now Miranda felt some very annoying tears forming in her eyes. "Bastable," she growled, "where are you? Where the *hell* are you?" Miranda! She could hear her parents' annoyed reactions, even though they weren't there. "Hell, hell, hell!" she yelled. Then she sighed. She couldn't just sit there the rest of the evening doing nothing, worrying about where Bastable was or whether or not he'd return.

Suddenly she heard a strange noise. It was distant, muffled, yet loud enough to startle her. It sounded like a hiss.

She glanced around the room. She knew it wasn't the radiator or the pipes because it was May and the heat wasn't on. The TV? No, that was turned off. She listened closely, but the sound was gone.

Miranda's mouth felt oddly dry, so she went to the kitchen for a glass of milk. She was on her second glass when Bastable came into her head again. *Milk,* she thought. *He adores milk.* She got another glass, filled it, and left it on the counter. Maybe I should leave a plate of cookies with it. He likes sweets too—especially if they're slightly stale. She reached up for the cookie jar.

Ssss came the sound again.

Miranda's hand froze in midair. Her skin prickled. "It's coming from my room," she said.

Slowly she walked down the hallway. With each step, the noise grew louder, nearer. *Maybe it's the wind,* she told herself. But she knew it wasn't windy out.

Her door was closed. She didn't remember closing it. The hiss was making it rattle and hum. Swallowing hard, Miranda grasped the doorknob. It felt icy cold. She shivered and dropped her hand. Suddenly, she let out her breath. "This is ridiculous," she said. "I'm being silly." Once again seizing the knob, which was now at least ten degrees warmer, she opened the door.

The noise stopped immediately. She switched on the light. Everything looked the same—her desk, her dresser, her bed. Nothing was out of place. She went over to her closet and flung open that door. She could see clear to the back, and there was nothing inside except her clothes, hung neatly as ever.

Maybe it's some kind of bug. A cicada or a katydid, she thought. But she vaguely recalled it wasn't the time of year for either one. She sat down on her bed for a while. *I wish Bastable would come back*, she thought sadly. Then she remembered the cookies.

She jumped up, heading for the door, and nearly tripped. "What the . . . " She looked down at her feet. Uncle Gerald's basket was lying there.

How did it get here this time? I know I put it over there just this afternoon, stupid thing. She picked it up, nearly threw it in its corner, and left the room.

She stopped in the kitchen, put Bastable's cookies on a plate, then went back to the living room where she watched TV for a long time with the sound off, making up her own dialogue for the succession of sitcoms and cop shows. At last, she decided she might as well go to bed. She brushed her teeth, washed her face, and turned out all but the front hall light. Then she padded to her room.

The door was open as she'd left it. With a small sigh of relief and fatigue, she walked inside and flicked on the light switch. But no light came on. With a bang, the door slammed shut behind her, and the hissing began again. There was no doubt this time where it was coming from. It was coming from the basket—shining like a small silver spaceship right on top of Miranda's bed.

She screamed. Her arms flailed out and her hand struck

her shelf. She grabbed a heavy book from it and heaved it at the basket. The hissing stopped. The glow faded. And the basket toppled to its side.

Then Miranda ran out of the room as fast as she could, raced down the hall into the bathroom, and locked the door. Wrapping herself in a towel, she crawled into the tub.

"I may be wrong," said a welcome voice some fifteen minutes later. "But I thought you humans fill that thing with water first before you take a bath."

CHAPTER 3

"Tell it to me once again—a bit slower this time. And it would help if you stopped shaking," Bastable said, perching on the side of the tub where Miranda was now sitting.

She took a deep breath and repeated, "It moved. The basket moved. And it hissed and glowed."

"Did you actually see it move?"

"I didn't have to see it move to know it did," Miranda told him, exasperation beginning to replace terror. "I put it in one place and a few hours later it was someplace else. I didn't touch it and there's nobody else who . . ." She broke off and glared at him suspiciously. "You haven't been playing some kind of practical joke, have you?"

"Kings are not known for playing jokes, practical or otherwise."

"I guess not." Miranda frowned and shivered again. "I need a sweater," she said. There was an old baggy one of her dad's lying on top of the hamper, though what it was doing there Miranda couldn't say. Bastable snatched it and tossed it to her.

"*Then* what happened?" he prompted as she slipped it on. "When you saw the basket hissing and glowing?"

"I threw a book at it," Miranda told him, "and it stopped."

"You didn't look inside?"

"What do you think I am, crazy? Would you look into a basket that sounded like it had some kind of serpent inside it?"

"Certainly," Bastable replied.

"Well then, you're the one who's crazy," Miranda snapped and hunched over, hugging her knees. A few moments later she said, "Where have you been anyway?"

"Hunting."

"For days?"

He nodded. "I needed to, as you humans put it, 'relieve stress.'"

"Did you catch a lot?"

"Let me see . . . I don't have my secretary here to tabulate the results, but I believe the accurate figures are . . ." He did a quick calculation. "Seventeen mice, five sparrows, two pigeons, and several goldfish. Although, technically, I suppose the goldfish don't count—they were already dead."

"Sorry I asked," muttered Miranda.

"What did you say?"

"I said, I thought you'd found a way back to Appledura and left," Miranda raised her voice.

Bastable regarded her solemnly. "Do you really think I would leave, Miranda, without even saying good-bye?"

"No," she answered softly, a bit ashamed. "I don't."

Bastable rose. "Good. Now let's go check out that basket."

"No way!" Miranda shouted.

"Now, Miranda," Bastable reasoned, sounding much more like a parent than a king, "you know you're going to have to go back to your room sooner or later. And when you get there sooner or later you're going to have to look inside that basket. I think it might as well be sooner."

Miranda had to admit that what he was saying sounded reasonable. She remembered too that her mother had cleaned the basket the other day and found nothing inside. But she was still frightened and so she hesitated.

"There's probably nothing inside anyway," Bastable went on. "I'll bet you imagined everything. You humans have very active imaginations. I've heard that some children even invent invisible playmates for themselves."

Miranda stared at him for a moment, then burst out laughing.

"What did I say to amuse you?" Bastable asked.

"N-nothing," Miranda sputtered through her guffaws. She was still giggling as she stood up and led them both to her room.

"So, this is it?" said Bastable, his furry brow furrowing.

Miranda hovered in the doorway, frowning. The basket was squatting in the corner of the room where Miranda had originally put it. It wasn't hissing. It wasn't glowing. And it certainly wasn't moving. Miranda didn't know whether to be thankful or somewhat disappointed.

"Come over here, Miranda. We'll look inside together."

The hair on Miranda's neck stirred as though someone had blown on it. "I don't think . . ." she began. Then she heard the click of a key turning in a lock. *Mom and Dad,* she realized. Quickly she scurried inside her room and shut the door. They'd come in in a few minutes, as they always did, to see if she was asleep. If they found her awake this late, they'd be annoyed. "Bastable, forget the basket. My parents are . . ."

But Bastable had already lifted the lid. "See," he said, rather triumphantly. "Just as I thought. There's nothing here. Come and look."

Miranda knew he would not be satisfied—and she would not be able to get into bed—until she obeyed him. Quickly, she joined him and peered down. "You're absolutely right," she agreed. "There's nothing there."

She'd barely finished the sentence when a long, sinuous body with a hooded head wrapped its coils around her arm and pulled her inside.

CHAPTER
4

"Where am I?" Miranda asked.

"In the basket," answered Bastable.

"Bastable! You're here too!"

"Of course. I jumped in after you."

"But that's impossible. How could you fit in here? How could *I* fit in here? It wasn't that big."

"I don't know. But it's comfortable enough—although it could use a cushion or two, preferably made of silk."

"So where are we?" Miranda asked again.

"I don't know, but I'd venture to guess it isn't your room."

Miranda shuddered. She'd venture to guess Bastable was right. "Where's the . . . snake?" she whispered.

"I believe it's gone."

"Did it bite you?"

"No."

"It didn't bite me either," Miranda murmured.

"Good. Then it is nothing to be afraid of."

"I wouldn't be so sure of that," said Miranda. In her mind flashed a glimpse of slitted amber eyes and a forked black tongue, and she shuddered again.

Then she heard a rustling noise. A slot opened above her head and a slice of greenish light striped her arm. "Bastable, what are you doing?" she asked.

"Getting out of this thing," the fenine replied, pushing the lid all the way off. "Are you coming with me?"

Scared as she was of leaving the basket, she was more unnerved by the thought of staying in it alone like some sort of trapped rabbit, ready to become either someone's dinner or pet. She grabbed hold of the edge of the basket and climbed out.

The ground was hard beneath her feet. Stone hard. Her legs trembled and threatened to buckle as she stood and peered around her. She was in some sort of cave lit only by a soft, eerie green phosphorescence on the walls and ceiling. Squinting, she could just see that the chamber she was in narrowed to a dimmer passageway.

"There are steps at the end," said Bastable, whose eyesight was keener than hers, especially in the dark. "We will have to climb them." He began to walk away.

"Wait." Miranda stopped him.

"What's the matter?"

She bit her lip, then said, "I've dreamed about having adventures, but not adventures like this."

"I wouldn't call this much of an adventure," said Bastable. "The time I battled the Mandragon of Fenopoly, now that was an adventure. And I was just a prince."

"Well, I'm just a kid," Miranda murmured.

But Bastable, whose ears were also sharper than hers, heard her. "That's the best time to start," he replied cheerily and padded down the passageway.

Miranda followed stiffly, trying not to stumble in the pale light, taking care not to brush the walls in case she encountered something unpleasant there. It didn't take long to reach the stairway. But to Miranda's dismay, she saw that it was long and very steep, the rough steps narrow and chipped.

Bastable noticed as well. "You have my permission to hold on to my tail," he granted graciously.

Without argument, Miranda grasped the tip and let the fenine guide her up the stairs. To her surprise he moved slowly and patiently instead of springing ahead the way he usually did.

When they reached the top, they found a door. Miranda pushed against it, but the heavy wood wouldn't budge. "What do we do now?" she asked.

Bastable didn't answer, and it was then Miranda realized she was no longer holding on to his tail. "Bastable! Bastable!" she cried, panic rising. "Don't leave me. Please don't leave me here alone."

Suddenly, the door swung open, and she nearly toppled into him. "Oh, Bastable, you scared me," Miranda blurted out. "I thought ... I don't know what I thought. . . ."

"The door was locked from the inside. I had to walk through to open it," he explained. "I believe we're in the main part of the building now. This is some sort of antechamber." He gestured around the room. It was sand-colored and plain, lit by a few well-placed torches. He led Miranda to one of the walls and pointed to some marks on it. "Do these look familiar to you?"

Miranda, who was trying to quiet her racing heart, forced herself to stare at them. "Yes," she said at last. "They look like the designs on the basket."

"What do you think they mean?"

Miranda shook her head. "I don't know."

"Well, perhaps we will soon find out."

Soon they stood before another door. "Stay here,

Miranda," Bastable told her so she wouldn't panic again. "I will go first."

But before he had a chance to move, the portal opened by itself and a brilliant golden light streamed out, blinding them both. When Miranda's vision at last cleared, she stared into the most beautiful and intimidating room she'd ever seen. Golden pillars supported an opalescent ceiling. Brocaded cushions littered an obsidian floor. At one end was a jade-green altar, at the other end, a canopied ruby-and-ebony throne. The throne was empty but the altar was covered with at least a hundred burnished statues—each one of them a snake. "Wow!" she exclaimed.

Bastable made a purring sound. Miranda turned to him and saw that the expression on his face was one of longing and delight. For a moment it banished her fear and awe. "Is this as good as your palace in Appledura?" she asked.

In answer, he purred again and entered the room. "I'd like to sit on that throne," he said, more to himself than to Miranda.

"I don't think that's a good idea," she told him.

"It'll just be for a moment," he replied, with a barely detectable whine.

"No!" Miranda shouted nervously.

Bastable turned to her. "Well, why not?"

Then they heard the hiss. And from the canopy, coils gleaming, eyes narrowed, hooded head held high, a very large cobra slithered down to the throne's brocaded seat and stared at them.

"That's why," Miranda tried to say, but all that came out was a squeak.

CHAPTER 5

"Welcome, King Bastable," said the snake, swaying slightly.

"It talks!" Miranda blurted.

"And friend." The cobra inclined gracefully toward her. In the center of its forehead was a single glittering ruby.

Miranda shrank back, wishing she hadn't drawn attention to herself, wishing even more she could run away. But she was rooted to the spot.

Unlike her, Bastable did not appear to be at all frightened of the creature. In fact, he seemed fascinated by it. "How interesting," he said. "You know our name. May we know yours?"

The snake raised its head high and spread its hood. "I am Naja, the Ever-Changing."

"This is a fine palace, Naja, the Ever-Changing. We have been admiring it."

"It is not a palace. It is a temple."

"Ah. Then you are a goddess."

"To some."

"We used to have a few gods and goddesses in Appledura, but they disliked the climate and they all left."

"But you, King Bastable, did not leave Appledura because of the weather."

"No, I didn't," Bastable said grimly. He fell silent.

So did the snake. Miranda, grown weary of her terror, burst out, "What do you want from us?"

Naja turned to her. "King Bastable's friend, what are you called?"

"You brought me here with him. How come you don't know my name too?"

"It was not in any of the visions."

"My name's Miranda and what visions?"

There was a pause, then Naja said, "Take my head in your hands and look into the jewel there, Miranda."

Miranda took a step backward. "I don't . . . I can't . . ."

"I will do it," offered Bastable.

"No, King Bastable. Let your friend. Do not be afraid, Miranda. Look into my jewel."

Slowly, Miranda moved toward the snake. She reached out to touch her, then pulled back her hands. "I can't . . ." She'd ceased to believe the snake would bite her, but she still didn't want to feel the scaly skin and the powerful jaws that held her deadly fangs.

Naja waited patiently, not speaking.

"I want to go home," she whispered and felt ashamed.

"Do you see this candle?" the snake nodded at a half-burned taper in a candlestick behind her. "When this has burned all the way down, I will send you home—if you still wish to go."

Miranda swallowed hard and again reached out her hands. She flinched but did not withdraw them as the cobra laid its head in her palms. She stared at the red jewel. It shimmered at her, small and sparkling. Then it began to grow until Miranda thought she was staring into a movie screen. At first there was nothing but crimson light. Soon shapes began to form and take on other colors. They became mountains and forests, cities and towns. People appeared—some smiling, some arguing good-naturedly, all going about their business. As Miranda watched, they moved through their day. Then as the sun set and the sky turned lilac, in each village, great or small, they gathered. Holding candles, clasping hands, they walked with measured pace to the temple there. Some worshiped Naja, the Ever-Changing. Others bowed to different gods. Their many paths led to one end—peace and contentment.

Then a haze clouded the scene, turbulent and gray. Miranda felt queasy. She had the urge to shut her eyes. But she couldn't. Soon the fog lifted and she saw a large army of men and women marching. They wore tunics bearing the likeness of a stern face with bright green eyes and carried whips with which they drove along a smaller, ragged band of people, bleeding and in chains. Through the town they tramped, and Miranda saw that every building there was razed and the temple was burnt to the ground.

Across the land the army rampaged until they came to the largest city Miranda had yet seen. The people there were better armed. They fought hard, but the army won. They stormed the temple there. With a gasp, Miranda recognized it. It was the very place where she now stood. But the pillars had buckled; the ceiling lay in shards; the altar was cracked in two; and the hundred golden statues were ground to dust under ten thousand angry heels.

Only the throne stood intact, though barren of rubies, and on it sat a new god whose bright green eyes said, "There is one path and one alone. Walk it—or you shall walk none at all."

"Horrible," Miranda whispered. "This is horrible. I don't want to see any more."

Immediately, the jewel went dark, and Miranda found herself gazing into Naja's amber eyes. For a long moment, she could not move, then she dropped her hands and shuddered. "Why did you make me look at that? What does it have to do with me or Bastable?"

"Yes," said Bastable. "What does it have to do with either of us?"

Miranda turned to look at him. "You saw it too?"

"Not all of it—I was watching over your shoulder—but enough."

"It is the future of my world—if the Charmer has his way," Naja told them.

"The Charmer? Who is he?" asked Bastable.

Naja hissed, baring her fangs. "My enemy—and yours."

Miranda felt a chill go up her spine, but Bastable seemed unmoved. "Please explain," he requested.

"He has many faces and many names, the Charmer. But his eyes remain the same. He travels from world to world, from future to past, and he can be in two worlds at the same time. But wherever he is, whenever he is, the Charmer devours souls. He will destroy my world—unless he is himself destroyed. You must help me destroy him."

"You must be crazy," Miranda scoffed.

Naja did not answer her.

In a reasonable voice, Bastable asked, "Why? Why should we help you?"

"Snare," Naja said.

A change came over Bastable. His tail stiffened; his hackles rose. He growled and his claws shot out. "Snare," he spat. "What do you know of Snare?"

"Snare is the Charmer," was Naja's reply.

Bastable and Naja stared at one another. Then, with determination, Bastable said, "Whatever must be done, I will do it. However long it takes, I will help you defeat the Charmer."

"Bastable! What are you saying? Who is this Snare? Why do you want to defeat him? And what about me? What am I supposed to do while you're on your quest?" Miranda cried.

"I can't tell you more now, Miranda," the fenine replied. "But you can come with us."

"Yes," said Naja. "The Correct Combination needs a human. You will do."

"The Correct Combination? *Will do?*" Miranda frowned.

"Six beings in all form the Correct Combination—and it is they and they alone who can conquer the Charmer. I am one. King Bastable is another. His name and where to find him I learned in shukor—what you call a trance. Your name I did not learn—nor the other three yet to come—only that at least one must be a human. You are a human, and you are here. So you will do. You *must* do."

Miranda turned to look at the candle. It was nearly

burnt out. The image of Naja's ruined world clung to her brain, and she did not want to part from Bastable, but to go with them? To battle an evil creature who had nothing to do with her? "You said when that candle burns out, if I still want to go you'll send me home. . . ." She dug her nails into her palms to stop herself from crying. "Well, I'm ready to go. Unless . . ." She paused. "Unless you give me one good reason why I must join you."

Naja rose to her full height. Her eyes flashed and her words dropped like venom from her mouth. "Because before the Charmer comes to my world, he will go to yours. He will devour the souls of your people. He will destroy your precious Earth."

CHAPTER
6

"Mumzum."

They were beneath the temple, in the phosphorescent cave. Naja had lit their way, her jewel shining like a beacon. Now the basket stood within its wavering circle of light, and Naja stood beside it, swaying slowly and humming. "Mumzum."

Maybe this time she won't have any visions, Miranda hoped, *any sign of who else is part of the Correct Combination. If we don't know whom we're looking for, we can't go flying away to fight the Charmer.* Bastable was beside her, silent, but with his tail curled lightly about her wrist. She guessed that he was trying to rub some of his bravery off on her. But it wasn't working. She felt foolish and scared.

Why am I going along with this? Just because a talking cobra who claims to be a goddess, for Heaven's sake, tells me some bozo she calls the Charmer and Bastable calls Snare—although he won't tell me what the creep did to him—is going to wreck my planet, and I might—mind you, not can, but might—be the human who's part of some bunch called the Correct Combination that can stop him, for that I'm actually going to get in that lousy basket and end up miles, maybe light years, from my home? I said Naja was crazy. I'm *the one who's nuts.*

Bastable's voice seemed to float out to her through the darkness, although he hadn't spoken at all. *You said you wanted adventure. . . .*

Miranda let out a shuddering sigh.

"Mumzum," Naja hummed, swaying now in wider circles. Her skin shivered all over. Her hood flared. "Mumzum. M*umȝum!*"

Suddenly, the snake stopped moving and stood rigid as a staff, her head pointing straight up. "Rattus!" she cried. And then, like a column of ash, she collapsed in a heap.

"Naja!" Miranda gasped and involuntarily stepped forward.

"I don't think you should touch her now," warned Bastable.

"I wasn't going to," Miranda shot back. But she did bend down to stare at the fallen snake. Naja's jewel glowed but faintly, and her tongue lolled out of one side of her mouth.

"Naja, are you all right?" Miranda asked quietly. She could never stand to see any animal hurt, not even one she didn't like.

The cobra lay still for what seemed a long time. Then she suddenly writhed once, nearly knotting her body in two, and, as if nothing strange had happened at all, she raised her head and commanded, "We will leave now." With startling speed, she slithered around Miranda's shaking knees up and into the basket.

Miranda stood up slowly and let out a groan.

"After you," said Bastable, gesturing to the basket.

"I think I'm going to throw up."

"Do it later when we arrive."

"Very funny."

"It wasn't a joke."

Miranda took several deep breaths and stared at the basket. *Okay, girl, this is it,* she told herself. *Forget your rabbit hole, Alice. The heck with fairy dust and Peter Pan, Wendy. And as for you, Dorothy, your tornado has nothing on this. We're off to fight the Charmer, the terrible Charmer of . . . everywhere.* Miranda's stomach gave a squeeze. She patted it. She could feel Bastable growing impatient. *All right, it's now or never.* Lifting her arms over her head like a diver, she took one more big breath. Then throwing back her head, she bellowed, "Last one in is a rotten egg," and jumped into the basket.

There was a faint bump. *We've arrived,* Miranda said to herself. The ride had been as smooth as the last one—a slight lift and then nothing at all. How long the flight was—or whatever it was the basket did—Miranda couldn't tell. It seemed like a few minutes, but she guessed it could just as well be a few millenia.

"How exactly does this conveyance work?" Bastable had asked in the close dark before they'd landed.

"Magic," Naja answered tersely, and he'd let it go at that. She did explain a bit about her visions. She said that although they always told her how to get to the place, they didn't always show it. Likewise, though she sometimes got a picture of the being the Correct Combination had to find, other times she learned just its name. This time she knew only that they had to find someone named Rattus.

"We are here," she said now. "Open the lid, Miranda."

Miranda hesitated. *I hope it's a nice place,* she thought. *Naja's temple wasn't bad. Maybe we'll be in a palace this time or a beautiful forest or a garden full of flowers. Exotic flowers I've never seen before.*

"Miranda," Naja repeated. "Open the lid."

Images of fragrant blossoms filling her head, Miranda obeyed. As the lid came away, she stood up and inhaled deeply—and was hit by the nastiest stench she'd ever encountered. "Whoo," she gagged. "Oh, disgusting."

"It is a bit strong," said Bastable.

"I'm not going out there," Miranda wheezed, burying her nose in the top of her turtleneck and plunking herself back down in the basket.

"I can help overcome the smell—if you will let me," suggested Naja.

"I'll let you all right," Miranda responded without further prompting. Even with her turtleneck over her nose, the smell still seeped in. "What do I have to do?"

"You must think of the fragrance you like best."

"That's easy enough," said Miranda. "Flowers . . . Wait. No. I've thought of something better. . . ."

"Keep thinking of it. Concentrate."

Eyes closed, Miranda pictured a pot on the stove. With a wooden spoon she was stirring the dark brown liquid bubbling in it. But the aroma wasn't right. . . . Then she felt something touch her forehead and she started.

"Keep thinking of the chocolate pudding," Naja whispered close to her face.

Miranda's eyes shot open. "How did you know what I—?"

"Close your eyes. Concentrate." Naja cut her off.

Miranda did as she was told. *Ping!* Something suddenly twinged in her forehead.

"Now," said Naja, "breathe deeply."

Her turtleneck still covering half her face, Miranda tentatively took a shallow breath. *Impossible*, she thought as the wisp of delicious odor wafted toward her. She slowly pushed down the turtleneck and inhaled more deeply. Yum. Someone somewhere was cooking up the most scrumptious and chocolaty batch of pudding she'd ever smelled. Miranda's stomach rumbled with hunger. She grinned. But the smile soon faded. "How did you do that?" she demanded of the snake.

"I did not do it. You did."

"What do you mean?"

"You had the thought. I merely helped it stay."

"You mean you hypnotized me?"

"I did nothing without your permission. Nor shall I."

"What are you talking about, you've done nothing without my permission? You dragged me into the basket. You took me to your world. You kidnapped me!"

"There was no other way to convince you to be part of the Correct Combination."

"You don't even know that I am for sure. You said so yourself. You just needed Bastable, and you got him by getting me."

"Miranda, this is no time to argue," Bastable put in. "You are here. You had the chance to go home, but you didn't take it. Now let's go."

Miranda had no argument for that, so she petulantly said, "Don't you want Naja to 'help' you smell something else, something like a barrel of mackerel or a truckload of trout? Or is this place fishy enough for you?"

"I would prefer a different odor. But I believe I'd better

not tamper with my olfactory function—it may come in handy."

Miranda ran out of things to say then. She was getting a quaky feeling in her knees again, and she had to breathe deeply once more to calm down. To her surprise the pudding smell was still there. Her outburst had not dissipated it. In fact, it was even stronger now. So strong that she began to believe that when she stepped out of the basket, it would be right into someone's kitchen. Before Naja or Bastable could ask her again, she did step out—right into a slimy puddle. She let out a yell and shook her foot viciously.

The stone floor wasn't the only thing that was wet. The dark, narrow walls and low, rounded ceiling were dripping too. It was as if the whole place was sweating.

"Another cave?" asked Bastable, glancing around.

"No. It is Under," said Naja, her jewel once again a beacon.

"You could call it that," Miranda said disgustedly as a couple of drops of rank liquid plopped on her head. "I have another name for it."

"What's that?" asked Bastable.

"Sewer."

"Sewer," the fenine mused. "What beings live in a sewer?"

"Alligators, according to some people." Miranda laughed harshly. "I don't believe them. The only beings I know that find a sewer as good as your palace are rats."

"Rats!" Bastable exclaimed. His back rippled with pleasure, and Miranda thought she saw him actually lick his lips.

Even Naja seemed agitated; her tongue flicked in and out rapidly, tasting the air.

Realizing he was being rather undignified, Bastable got hold of himself, but Miranda could see that the tip of his tail still twitched. "Rats are a great delicacy in Appledura," he explained. "We call them *platis do ros*—kings' dish. It's been a very long time since I've sampled it."

"I had several last week," Naja said conversationally, sounding most ungoddesslike. "Do you catch them yourself, or are they presented to you?"

"Oh, I catch them. Without the hunt, there is no pleasure in such a dish."

"I agree."

"I think you're both gross," said Miranda, forgetting their ranks.

Naja turned to her. "Do not worry. If there are any such inhabitants here, we shall not disturb them."

"We won't?" Bastable drooped. "Why not?"

"We may need their help. We will not receive it if we eat them."

"Help? From a bunch of rats?" said Miranda. "What kind of help can those dirty animals give?"

Suddenly, Bastable dropped on all fours. He sniffed the air. His ears pricked. His back arched. His tail waved wildly.

"We are about to find out," said Naja.

Miranda turned slowly. There in front of her and her companions swarmed a huge army of sharp-toothed, red-eyed rats—and they looked as if they meant business.

CHAPTER
7

Miranda was standing perfectly still and thinking about pajamas. She was glad that she wasn't wearing them. *They wouldn't stand up to rat teeth*, she thought. At least her loose-fitting pants, turtleneck, and her dad's baggy sweater were a little tougher. *It'll take the rats at least a minute to bite through them—instead of ten seconds*, she told herself, and shuddered.

As for Naja and Bastable, they had no clothes at all, but they did have formidable weapons. Miranda had nothing—just her feet and fists, which, in her opinion, were pretty useless. *We could run or get in the basket and take off*, she thought. But somehow she didn't think her companions would go for either idea.

Next to her, Bastable growled low in his throat. The rats were shuffling forward. Miranda clenched her fists. Her whole body stiffened, preparing for the onslaught.

Suddenly, Naja opened her mouth and let out three sharp squeaks, like descending notes on a horn. The rats stopped, staring. Naja repeated the cries, this time ending them in a long, rolling *chur*.

There was a lengthy pause. Then slowly a single rat detached himself from the mass and came forward. He was an elderly rat. His muzzle had gone white and he moved haltingly. "You have spoken my language. Now I'll speak yours. Why have you invaded our home?" he asked, his high voice wavery.

"We seek someone. Our search has led us here," Naja told him.

"Who is it you're looking for?"

"Rattus."

The rat army erupted in a series of scuffles and muffled squeaks. Like a general sure of his troops, the old rat silenced them with one squeal, never taking his small eyes off Naja. "What do you want with him?" he asked.

"We need his help."

"Help? With what?"

"With the Charmer."

"Who is that?"

Instead of a long explanation, Naja said, "A great enemy—ours and yours."

The aged rodent cocked his head. "It seems to me we can't have any enemy greater than a cat—"

"A *fenine*. A fenine *king*." Bastable growled again.

"—and a snake," the rat finished, ignoring Bastable. Behind him his comrades squeaked rapidly in agreement, then began to advance.

"Wait!" shouted Miranda in desperation.

"Who's speaking?" the rat general squinted weak eyes at her and wrinkled his pointed nose. "Ah, Enemy Number Three—a human."

"I'm . . . I'm n-not your enemy," Miranda stammered. "And neither are they. I'm a human, yes. And I'm afraid of you—and of snakes too. But Naja told me . . . *showed* me . . . what the Charmer will do to her world. He'll do it to mine too. So I'm here. Now please, if you know where Rattus is, take us to him."

The rat hesitated, still squinting. Then he took a step

forward. The others moved with him, but he turned his head and stopped them with a harsh squeak. Deliberately, he trudged his way to Miranda's feet, where he paused to catch his breath. Then, with a remarkable burst of speed, he scuttled up her body all the way to her shoulder. She jumped and flailed at him. From his crouch, Bastable sprang, claws shooting out, and made a grab.

"No!" Miranda warned him, dropping her own hands. "Don't hurt him!"

The old rat, clinging precariously to her shoulder, stuck his whiskers in her face. "I'm tired," he said, panting. "Old and tired. You, human, will give me a ride."

"To where?" Miranda said, wincing.

"To rescue Rattus. Where else?"

"Wait, the basket. What should we do with it?" Miranda asked Naja.

But it was the rat general who answered, "Let the cat carry it."

"*Fenine*," Bastable snarled.

"I'd better carry it," Miranda said quickly. Stooping carefully so the rat could keep his balance, she picked it up. "Maybe you'd prefer to sit on the lid," she told him.

"I prefer your shoulder." The rat's lips pulled back slightly, as though he were grinning, to reveal teeth that were worn to stumps. Miranda was grateful that she could still smell chocolate pudding, because she had a distinct feeling that the general's breath was less than sweet.

"Suit yourself," she said brusquely and began to walk. Bastable and Naja kept pace with her, while behind, like a great shadow, moved the rat army.

No one spoke as they marched, except the general, and that was only to order "Left" or "Right" or "Go straight." The sound of their feet pattering on stone or splashing through water echoed loudly off the narrow walls.

Miranda could not believe there were so many twists and turns to the dank sewer. Each time they rounded a bend, Miranda prayed they'd reached the end. But they hadn't. Soon she began to wonder if there was an end. She could barely feel her feet: She couldn't tell if they were warm or cold, wet or dry. In a flash of sympathy, she wondered if Bastable's feet bothered him too, or poor Naja's belly. *If this were a bus ride, Jason and Fred and some of the other kids would have sung "One Hundred Bottles of Beer on the Wall" at least one thousand times by now*, she thought, recalling her classmates back home.

Back home. She wasn't certain how she knew this wasn't home; she just did. *It must be Sunday there by now*, she said to herself. *Mom and Dad must be frantic. They've probably called the cops.* A wave of worry and homesickness crashed inside her. Tears welled up in her eyes. *At least you won't have to go to school tomorrow*, she told herself bleakly. Then aloud she complained, "We've been walking for hours."

"Nearly there," the general replied.

But it was another half hour or so before he abruptly commanded, "Stop. Up there." He shinnied down Miranda's side to the ground.

She looked up. There seemed to be some kind of ladder up ahead. A metal ladder set against the wall. It led up to a manhole, covered with a metal lid.

"How are we going to get that off? It's solid iron or steel or whatever they make those things out of," she said. She suddenly felt as floppy as a scarecrow. She could barely hold the basket or even stand up straight.

"I will open it," said Naja.

"What?" Miranda yawned. Her stomach rumbled. *Now I really am hungry.* She licked her lips. *And thirsty too.* "How can you do that? You don't even have arms."

In answer, Naja rose up. "Imzim," she hummed, aiming her jewel at the manhole cover.

"Stealth and silence will be your best tactics up there," the old rat said. "Never let your enemy know you're here."

Miranda looked at him. It was the first time he'd actually sounded concerned.

"Don't worry, rodent," sneered Bastable. "When a fenine king stalks, not even a ten-eared otiol can hear him."

"What you find up there will have sharper hearing than a *twenty*-eared otiol—whatever that is—cat."

"Insolent vermin," Bastable snapped. "I'll show you what *sharp* means." But before he could carry out his threat, an explosion shook the sewer and the manhole cover sailed away like a Frisbee.

Miranda gasped. Bastable let out a yowl. All the rats squeaked.

"So much for stealth and silence," Miranda said when she caught her breath.

Naja ignored her and slithered up the ladder. She waited a full minute until she said, "It is safe."

"After you, Miranda," Bastable said as he had before,

but his eyes were not on her. Instead, they glared at the general.

"No, Bastable. After you," Miranda responded and gave him a slight but rude shove with the basket.

He growled faintly, but sprang up the ladder.

Right behind him climbed Miranda. It was a bit tricky with the awkward basket, but she was managing. She no longer felt limp. The explosion had taken care of that. When she reached the third rung, she turned and looked down. The general and his army were still there, watching. *They helped us,* she thought. *They don't like us any more than we like them, but they did help.* "Why did you agree to lead us here?" she asked.

The old rat twitched his whiskers once. "Rattus is our friend. He needs your help—and you need his."

"He's in danger?"

"Yes. We all are. Our numbers are dwindling. Each day more of us disappear. No one returns to tell us why."

"Rattus is gone too?"

"Yes."

"Then it may be too late."

"It may be. But it may not be. Rattus is stronger, braver, more clever than most, with a talent for spying and the wits to avoid getting caught at it."

"But still he disappeared."

"Yes. But perhaps by choice."

And perhaps not, Miranda added silently. She sighed, repositioned the basket, and cleared her throat. "Thanks." She felt a salute would be appropriate, but nodded curtly instead.

The general bobbed his grizzled head. "Good luck, human," he replied. Then he about-faced his army and marched them away.

Miranda watched them melt into the sewer's gloom. *It's as though they've never been here at all,* she thought. Then she turned, gritted her teeth, and climbed up the rest of the ladder.

CHAPTER
8

Whatever Miranda had expected, it wasn't this. A street, yes. But not this kind of street. It seemed to be in a suburb. There was grass bordering the wide asphalt—if that's what the pinkish material was. There were also bushes and a few spiky trees. But there were no houses. There was only one long, low, flat-topped building. It seemed to be made of metal, but not any kind Miranda had ever seen on Earth.

What is it, Miranda wondered. *A prison?* But there were no bars on the windows. In fact, there were no windows. *A hospital,* she asked herself. *A school? A factory? Do they have those in this place?*

"I'll go in first, as a scout," Bastable said, with some relish. He had not been one since he was quite young—in the Appledurian tradition of Basic Training, which even heirs to the throne had to undergo.

"No. I think we should not yet separate," said Naja.

"You want us all to go in together? Bastable is invisible, but you and I will be noticed," Miranda said.

"No. You will be seen, but not noticed."

"How do you know?"

"I sense it."

Miranda paused. "What about the basket?"

"Hide it in one of the bushes."

"What about you? You mean to say you won't be noticed either?"

"I would be noticed if I were visible."

"You can make yourself invisible too?" Bastable put in.

"No, not here. Only in my world—or in the basket."

"Then what are you going to do?" Miranda asked. Her stomach was grumbling more insistently now, and her fatigue was beginning to return.

"I shall wrap myself about your waist, under your sweater—with your permission, of course."

"Of course," Miranda replied sarcastically. But she was thinking, *Well, I've already held that snake's head and had a grubby rat sit on my shoulder. How much worse could this be?* She sighed. "All right." After hiding the basket in a thick bush, she pulled up her sweater and hunkered down.

The snake slid up her leg to her waist and wrapped herself snugly around.

Some people like Suzanne and Amy Beth would love to have a snakeskin belt—minus the rest of the snake, thought Miranda, and she let out a hoot of laughter.

"It would not be wise to draw attention to yourself," Naja warned, her voice muffled by the heavy cotton.

Setting her face in a serious expression, Miranda said, "You're absolutely right," and followed Bastable to the door.

It was unlocked, and it led them into a long gray corridor bright with fluorescent lights. There were many doors along the hall. Miranda didn't know which, if any, to enter.

Suddenly, a middle-aged woman appeared. She was tall and thin, and her eyes were gray and cool. It took Miranda a minute to realize she hadn't simply materialized, but had come from a room off to the left.

"Trance Tech?" she asked.

Miranda had no idea what she meant, but she took a chance and nodded.

"Better hurry, my dear. It's starting. You don't want to be late." The woman paused, wrinkling her nose. "Dear, what happened to your shoes?"

Miranda looked down. Her feet were sopping wet and somewhat aromatic. "I . . . uh . . . stepped in a . . . puddle."

It was obvious that the woman didn't know whether or not to believe her. But politely she said, "Oh, dear. What a shame. I hope you don't catch cold. Well, hurry along."

"Where is the . . . uh . . ."

"Room twenty-three B, second floor. Go up this staircase and turn right. You can't miss it."

"Thank you," said Miranda. As she headed for the staircase, she muttered, "Not noticed, huh?"

Naja did not respond.

"Here it is. Twenty-three B," she said when she found the room. She opened the door. A few heads turned incuriously her way and just as nonchalantly turned back. A bunch of people were seated in an amphitheater of some kind. On the stage below, a small bald man with a professorial air stood at a lectern. Next to him, on a table, was a large, empty cage, visible to everyone in the audience. Miranda took the nearest empty seat, Bastable the one next to it. Miranda hoped no one would try to take that seat. Bastable could not be seen, but he could be felt.

"The subcortical implant introduced to the medulla oblongata induced great calmness and placidity in several specimens even when they were severely threatened. Do not mistake this for mere tranquilization. The specimens were not simply tranquilized. They were hypnotized. The advantage over normal hypnosis is that the subject need not be suggestible. The implant works on anyone."

"What is he talking about?" Bastable murmured in her ear.

"I don't know," she mouthed. She felt Naja tighten around her waist, but the snake said nothing, and Miranda didn't dare speak to her.

On and on the little man droned. Miranda's eyes grew heavy. She tried to keep them open by glancing around the amphitheater. The audience was young, too young for this kind of lecture, she realized. It was also . . . what was the word . . . rapt—glassy eyed and slack jawed. Miranda found it both funny and disturbing.

Next to her, Bastable let out a little snore. She fought down a giggle, glad no one else could hear him. A few minutes later she too began to drowse. She was nearly asleep when, from far off, she heard the professor say, "You will now see a dramatic presentation of what I have been discussing."

Naja gave her another squeeze, which woke her. She blinked down at the stage. The little man was lifting up a small cage and dumping its contents into the big one. The contents were one brown rat. Miranda sat up suddenly and stared at the rodent, which was scampering about the cage, sniffing, searching for food.

"This is a completely untrained Terranian rat," the professor said. He bent down and picked up a carrying case. From it he removed a skinny orange cat.

"Looks a bit like my cousin," Bastable said, yawning. He was still sleepy and didn't know exactly what was going on. "Only smaller, of course. And badly in need of a good wash. You know, whether you live in a palace or a ... *sewer*, there's never any excuse for poor grooming. . . ."

"Be quiet, Bastable," Miranda shushed him under her breath so no one would hear. Her belly was tingling unpleasantly, and not with hunger. The feeling worsened as she watched the man open the big cage and lower the cat inside, holding it firmly by the neck. The cat, spying the rat, laid back its ears and growled. The rat rushed into a corner and began to dig frantically.

Don't. Oh, don't, Miranda begged silently, holding her breath. She let it out with relief when the man, obeying, lifted out the cat and put it back in the carrying case.

"Notice the rat's typical flight reaction," he said. He got a net and scooped it out and back into its cage. He put that cage down on the floor and lifted up another, which contained a different rat. Miranda's fear returned more violently than before. "Now, an implanted specimen," said the professor, dumping it in the cage, where it too began to sniff and scrounge. "Watch carefully." His voice had an edge to it now, a touch of the magician's dramatic flair, which he hadn't previously displayed.

Once again he lowered the orange cat and held it in the rat's cage.

Once again, the cat laid back its ears and growled. But this rat ignored the feline. As Miranda watched with awful fascination, it scampered about blithely—closer and closer to its mortal enemy.

"Ridiculous," sneered Bastable. "Unsporting." He was wide awake now, and though his tone was disdainful, his ears were laid back just like those of the cat in the cage.

Still closer danced the rat. Miranda gripped her chair's armrests. She wanted to look away, but she was transfixed. So was everyone around her. The little man made a slight movement. For a second, Miranda thought that he was going to lift out the excited tom which was quivering with hunger and blind instinct. But instead, he loosened his grip and let the cat go.

Something let go in Bastable as well. "Attack!" he yelled as the cat sprang, knocking down the rat with one swipe of its paw.

"No!" Miranda screamed, jumping to her feet.

Heads turned her way. Beneath her sweater, Naja squeezed hard enough to make her grunt. Miranda slapped at her and let out a sob.

On the stage below, the rat dangled, legs waving slowly, from the cat's jaws. A moment later, it was still. The cat set it down and began to feast. But Miranda was no longer watching it. Tears rolling down her cheeks, she was pushing her way through the seats and out to the aisle. As she reached the door, the audience broke into applause. "Bravo, Professor N-Chant!" it yelled at the little man. "Bravo!"

Miranda ran out into the hall, banging at doors until she found the ladies' room. Bastable followed, running on all fours to keep pace. Miranda locked them both in a stall and sat down, shaking and weeping. "Horrible! That was horrible!"

"Well, it certainly lacked finesse," Bastable said, trying to comfort her.

He failed. "You seemed to enjoy it well enough," she snapped.

"I regret my reaction. I assure you it was involuntary," he told her.

Miranda relented. "It wasn't your fault, Bastable. You couldn't help it any more than that cat could. It was that man's fault. That creepy little professor. Why'd he do that? Who is he?"

Her head poking absurdly from under Miranda's sweater, Naja's amber eyes stared up into Miranda's reddened ones. "That creepy little professor," she said slowly, "is the Charmer, and he has just demonstrated the means by which he will control this world."

CHAPTER 9

"Then we're too late," said Miranda after a long silence.

"You mean that was Rattus..." Bastable's voice trailed off.

"No," Naja interrupted. "I would know if Rattus had died."

"Where is he then?"

"He is here, in this laboratory. But where I do not know."

"We have to find him, and quickly."

"Shh," warned the snake.

The rest room door had opened. There was a babble of voices and a scuffle of feet. Then stall doors banged on either side of Miranda.

"Isn't it exciting?" babbled one voice. "He's going to let us watch the implantation tonight. The subject is supposed to be especially wily. It's already gotten out of its cage twice."

"Well, we are the privileged ones, aren't we?" a second, smugger voice, said. "Chronologically, children. Mentally, superior to ninety-nine point seven percent of the population. We hold the future in our hands. We *are* the future."

There were several giggles and votes of approval. Then the first girl spoke again. "I think Ms. R-Type's in love with him."

"Ms. R-Type's always in love with somebody," said the smug voice. "And so are you."

"I am not, Patsy P-Body."

Someone banged on Miranda's stall. "Hey, is anyone in there? I've gotta go."

Miranda started, but didn't answer.

"Someone's there. I see her feet."

"Are you okay in there?"

"Say yes," Naja whispered.

"I'm fine," Miranda called.

"Then hurry up, will you? I don't want to have an accident on the floor."

Miranda opened the stall door slowly. A figure rushed past her inside, nearly slamming the door on Bastable's tail. He gave the girl a disgusted look and threaded his way to the door, where he waited for Miranda.

A couple of girls laughed at their classmate's haste. Another girl, big-boned and beefy, laid a restraining hand on Miranda's arm. "Say, weren't you the kid who ran out of Professor N-Chant's lecture. You ought to go see Ms. A–Range. She'll straighten you out."

"No. No, I'm not . . . I didn't . . ." Miranda stammered.

The girl, who had tiny eyes set in a square face, made her eyes even smaller. "Yeah? Well, I was sitting right nearby and you sure look like her."

"Excuse me," said Miranda, shaking off the girl's hand and hurrying out the door. There was a telephone cubicle nearby. At least that was what Miranda guessed it was—the glassy tubes that were hanging there with discs on each end did not resemble any phone she'd ever used. Huddling inside it with her companions, she said, "The clever subject they were talking about, the one that's going to get implanted tonight, that's got to be Rattus."

"I believe you are right," said Naja.

"If the implantation's tonight we don't have a minute to lose. Once they put that thing in his brain, he won't be of any use to the Correct Combination, will he?" Miranda went on, sounding deliberately hard, but feeling pudding-soft inside.

"He will not—and the Correct Combination will be of no use to my world—or either of yours."

"Then let's stop standing around here," said Bastable impatiently. "Let's go find him."

"I think this time we should split up. It'll be faster that way," suggested Miranda.

"Yes, I agree," Naja said. "You can search this floor. King Bastable can take the first one. I will go to the lowest level underground."

Miranda's palms began to sweat. She did not mean or expect the snake to leave her too. Bastable turned to her. "It will be dangerous. You are unarmed," he said.

"I'll be all right," said Miranda with much more confidence than she felt. "I look like I fit in here." In fact, she wanted to find the rat and get out of this nasty building, this dismal world as quickly as possible.

Bastable did not argue further with her. "Let's meet out by the basket when we've each finished the search." He turned to go.

But Naja stopped him. "Your Highness, if either of us

finds Rattus, we will, of course, refrain from making him our dinner," she reminded him.

Bastable cast her a look that was half offended, half sheepish. "We will refrain," he said haughtily, and loped away.

Naja slid down to the floor. "If you need me, call," she told Miranda, then slithered into the vent on the wall and disappeared.

It was only after the tip of her tail vanished from view that Miranda realized Naja had not spoken the words aloud. *But I'm sure I heard them*, she thought. *Oh, well. Never mind. Where do I begin?* How *do I begin?* She peered down the length of the hall. It was empty. *Come on, Miranda*, she tried to give herself encouragement. *What could happen to you here? The Charmer—if Naja's right and that little professor really is the Charmer—he's not interested in you. He doesn't know who you are. Nobody does. They all think you're one of this bunch of kid scientists. So just act the part. You can do it. You were great as the littlest pig in* The Three Little Porkers—*even if that was way back in second grade.*

Easing herself into the corridor, Miranda decided it was best to look purposeful. She opened the first door she came to. It was a supply closet. The second door led to a small office, but nobody was there. The third opened into a conference room. It had one occupant—a man feeding a blue chair cushion into the wide mouth of an odd-looking cylindrical machine. There was a lot of gurgling and sucking. Then the machine spit out the cushion. It was now bright green. The man replaced the cushion on the chair and took up a second one. Then he noticed Miranda and smiled blankly.

"Pardon me, but I'm looking for the room where the animals are held," she said.

The man kept smiling, but didn't say a word.

"The animals for Professor N-Chant's . . . uh . . . experiments," she went on. When he still said nothing, she asked, "Do you understand me?"

"Of course," the man answered in a flat voice and fed the second cushion to the machine.

Miranda felt the muscle in her cheek twitch. The man gave her the willies. He reminded her of the rat, the one the cat had caught. He looked at her now with blue eyes as bland as his voice. "Then where is the room?" she asked.

"Professor N-Chant is a genius," he responded. He smiled again and neatly caught the cushion the machine had just spit out.

"Don't let me keep you from your redecorating," Miranda snapped and flung open the door.

But she just as quickly closed it again. Out in the hall was the big girl from the ladies' room and two of her friends.

Miranda waited till she thought they were gone and cracked the door once again. *Safe*, she told herself. Then a door at the end of the hall opened and a young man in a white lab coat came out. He was holding a small cage with a rat inside. *Eureka*, Miranda cheered silently—and headed that way. She was nearly there when a hand landed heavily on her shoulder. She jumped, but caught hold of herself. That girl with the piggy blue eyes again. She turned, running over what to say in her head, and looked up instead into a pair of cool gray ones. It was the tall, thin woman she'd met on her way to the lecture. The woman smiled, and her lips were thin as well.

"I've been looking for you, my dear," she said. "I saw you leave the amphitheater."

"Oh. Well. I . . ."

"There's no need to explain. Let's go to my office, shall we?"

"I . . . I wanted . . . I'd like to see the . . . uh . . . specimen first. The one that's going to get . . . implanted."

"There will be plenty of time for that. We don't want you to distress yourself again, do we?"

"I'm not distressed . . . not now. . . . I mean . . . not anymore . . . Professor N-Chant is a genius, isn't he?"

"I'm glad you feel that way, my dear. It will make the procedure even more pleasant."

"The procedure?" Miranda swallowed. "What procedure?"

But all the woman said was, "Come this way." She led Miranda around the corner, down another hall, and into a room. A secretary sat at a desk. "Two telephases for you, Ms. A-Range," she said.

"Tell them I'll get back to them. I have more important business." She smiled again at Miranda.

The corner of Miranda's lip spasmed.

Ms. A-Range saw it. "Don't worry, dear," she assured. "This won't hurt a bit." Then she ushered Miranda into another room. The walls were the same color as the woman's eyes. "Have a seat." She motioned Miranda to a chair.

Miranda sat. So did Ms. A-Range, in front of a computer terminal. "What is your name?"

Miranda paused. Her throat was dry and she coughed. "Um. Mmmm. Patsy," she choked out at last. "Patsy P-Body."

"Ah, yes," said Ms. A-Range. "And your instructor?"

"Ms. . . . R-Type."

"Now, Patsy, have you been under any stress lately?"

Miranda nearly laughed, but she forced down the giggles. "No," she answered soberly.

"Have you been ill?"

"No."

"Have you changed your sleeping or eating habits?"

In answer, Miranda's stomach gave a loud grumble. "I've always had a good appetite, Ms. A-Range," she said with a small smile.

"Yet you were upset by Professor N-Chant's breakthrough experiment. Strange. Your file does not indicate any past sensitivity. Well, never you mind. A bit of desensitizing and you'll be fine." She stood up and laid her hand on the wall. A panel slid open without the slightest sound. Miranda had no choice but to follow.

The panel led to another gray room. But this one had no desk or chair, only a padded table with a small humming box next to it.

"Lie down, Patsy, and make yourself comfortable," said Ms. A-Range. "A marvelous machine, this. One of Professor N-Chant's finest inventions. It will eliminate any psychological disturbances you have."

"Oh, no . . . I . . . that is . . . I don't have any disturbances." Miranda backed away toward the door.

Her gray eyes hard, Ms. A-Range held up a small black
tube and pointed it at a spot above Miranda's head.
"Don't make me use the Shower Stun," she said.

"All right." Gingerly, Miranda got up on the table and
stretched out.

"Now, I shall clip these on. . . ." Ms. A-Range snapped
bracelets over Miranda's wrists. The bracelets were attached to the table so that she could not get up.

"What are these for?" Miranda asked, growing more
frightened by the minute.

"In case you fall asleep, Patsy. We wouldn't want you
to fall off the table and hurt yourself." Then Ms. A-Range
pulled out a pair of earphones attached to the machine.

"How long do I have to stay here?"

"Oh, overnight should do it."

"Overnight! But my . . . my . . . parents . . ."

"I'll call them." She slipped the earphones on Miranda's
head. "There." Flicking on the switch, she smiled. "Relax,
dear." She patted Miranda's leg. "You'll thank me for this
tomorrow." Then she left the room.

A low note thrummed in Miranda's ears. She struggled
to move her hands, but to no avail. She was trapped.
"Bastable, Naja," she cried. She didn't care if Ms.
A-Range heard her. She was terrified. "Help me! Help
me!" The note grew louder. It was like a silver probe,
searching out one section of her brain. But it was not
unpleasant. "Help me! Help me!" Miranda yelled again,
but the words, the feeling had less urgency.

Soon nothing had urgency. She did not need any help.

The rat did not need to leave the cage. It was happy. Miranda was happy. She was going to be happy forever and ever. Professor N–Chant *was* a genius. Miranda had no doubt about that. No doubt at all.

CHAPTER

10

Attack heh heh heh. Attack heh heh heh. Attack heh heh heh. The words kept stuttering in Miranda's head—a phonograph needle stuck in a groove. She wasn't happy now. She was annoyed. "Stop it," she mumbled. And the words did, only to be replaced by a horridly warped and distorted version of "Pop Goes the Weasel," a song Miranda inexplicably had always found frightening.

"Stop it!" She raised her voice.

Something touched her forehead. The song screeched to a halt and made her eyes fly open. But they wouldn't focus. Everything was smeary, like a lens coated with Vaseline. Miranda felt a weight on her chest. She couldn't make out what it was. She tried to rub her eyes to see it, but her hands wouldn't move. *Where am I? What's going on?* she wondered groggily.

At last her vision cleared, and she saw that the weight on her chest was a snake. "N . . . N . . ." The name was on the tip of her tongue, but it wouldn't come off.

"Is she all right?" said a voice. It didn't come from the serpent.

"B . . . B . . . Bastable!" She thrust out the word. It was as good as saying "Open, Sesame"; it magically unlocked her brain.

"I'm here," he said, coming to her side.

"She is all right now," the cobra responded to the fenine.

"And Naja," Miranda recalled. "What happened to me? I remember this humming noise. . . . A woman . . . I can't remember her name. . . . She hooked me up to this thing. . . ." She paused, blinking. "How did you find me? How did you know where I was?"

"You called for help," answered the cobra.

"You heard me?"

"Not with my ears."

"Do snakes have ears?" asked Bastable curiously.

Naja didn't answer him. But Miranda said, "Bastable, did you hear me too, with your ears or otherwise?"

"No," answered the fenine. "But I heard Naja. She was in the room directly above mine. We talked through the vent. She told me you were in trouble and where to go. I got those earphones off your head and shut off the machine. She did something or other to wake you up."

"That woman, she'll be back. We'd better get out of here," urged Miranda. "Can you get these off?" She knocked her wrists against the bracelets. "She . . . pushed something over by my feet, I think."

"This?" Bastable pressed a button.

The bracelets sprang open and Miranda jumped off the table. "I think I know where Rattus is. Naja, you'd better get under my sweater."

But before Naja did, the panel slid open and Miranda's gray-eyed captor entered. She gaped at the unfettered girl and the rearing snake, but was peculiarly unafraid. "What is this? What is going on? Who turned off the machine? And how did this specimen get in here?" She fired off questions as she blocked the exit.

Naja hissed and bared her fangs. Miranda ordered, "Let us pass and we will not harm you, Ms. ... Ms. ... De-range ... Strange ..."

"A-Range."

"Oh, yes."

Bastable had other ideas. "Strike, Naja, or she will set the guards on us."

"I didn't see any guards," said Miranda.

"I did."

"Who are you talking to, my dear?" asked Ms. A-Range.

Naja feinted at her like a swordsman, but the woman stood unfazed.

Suddenly, Miranda knew why. "You ... you and the ... the ... janitor and who knows who else ... you've been *implanted.*"

"Professor N-Chant is a genius," Ms. A-Range replied with a smile. She moved toward a small mesh square on the wall. It resembled a speaker.

"Strike, Naja!" Bastable cried. "If you won't, I shall."

"No!" shouted Miranda. In one motion she seized a black tube from the counter, aimed it at the ceiling above the woman, and pressed the red disc on its end. A stream of pencil-thin rays of white light poured down. Ms. A-Range let out a long, contented sigh and crumpled to the floor.

"What was that?" Bastable asked, standing over the woman's form.

"I think she called it the Shower Stun."

"How long will it last?"

"I don't know."

"It may not be long enough. Naja had better . . ."

"I can use another method," interrupted the snake. She slithered to Ms. A-Range and touched the woman's forehead with her jewel. "You will remember nothing," she said.

There was a tiny flash of red light. Ms. A-Range sighed again and curled up in a ball.

"Now," said the cobra, rising and encircling Miranda's waist once again, "we go. Miranda, lead the way."

Miranda was able to get the panel open, and the group exited into Ms. A-Range's office. But Miranda had forgotten about the secretary at the desk in the next room.

The young woman looked up, puzzled. "Aren't you the girl who's being desensitized?" she asked.

"Professor N-Chant is a genius," Miranda replied.

The secretary smiled. "Yes, he is."

Miranda smiled back and edged out the door. "This way," she told Bastable, hurrying them both to where she guessed Rattus was being held.

Bastable slipped in first while Miranda and Naja waited in the hall. He was not gone long. When he came out, he did not look pleased. "There's no one there," he said. "No humans. No rats. No creatures at all."

"But I saw someone carry in a rat in a cage," Miranda insisted.

"Well, it isn't there now."

"Maybe there's another room behind it—like in Ms. A-Range's office."

"I checked. There isn't."

Miranda frowned. Then she noticed a figure in a white coat at the end of the corridor. He was carrying a cage. "Bastable, follow that man," Miranda ordered.

Without pausing to chide her for issuing commands to a king, Bastable took off. Miranda hurried after him, trying to look determined but not desperate. She hovered several doors away at a bulletin board on which the only posted items were a schedule of upcoming lectures and demonstrations and a layout of the building labeling restrooms, telephases, and shelters. "These Shelters Are to Be Occupied Only in the Event of Morphite Attack," read the words under the chart. *I hope I never find out what a Morphite Attack is*, thought Miranda.

She heard soft footsteps behind her. Out of the corner of her eye she could see the white-coated man walking away. His arms were empty. A moment later, the door behind her opened and Bastable stood on the threshold. He was trying to appear composed, but Miranda noticed that his claws kneaded the air and there was a faint but noticeable strand of saliva trickling out of one corner of his mouth.

"I believe we've found him," he said.

Miranda—and Naja—walked swiftly into the room. A dim bar of violet light glowed over rows of cages filled with rats of all shapes and colors. One cage, set apart from the rest, was wrapped in a fine web of green wire. Miranda reached out her hand toward it.

"Don't touch it unless you don't mind being fried," came a scratchy voice from within.

Miranda jerked back.

A narrow snout appeared, topped by a pair of bright beady eyes. "Switch is under the counter," said the rat.

Miranda fumbled until she found and flicked it. There was no visible sign that anything had been shut off.

"Okay, you can open it now."

"Rattus?" said Miranda as she opened the cage door.

"Yeah, that's me. I don't know who sent you, but thanks. I'll return the favor someday if I can. . . . Hey, your buddy over there is drooling. Get him in a bear hug or something until I blow this joint, okay?"

Bastable wiped at his mouth. "I have sworn a king's oath to keep you safe."

"Yeah? That's nice," Rattus tossed out as he dropped from the cage to the counter. Then, in a loud whisper, he said to Miranda, "What loony bin did you spring him from?"

"Are all the rats here such disrespectful louts?" Bastable hurled back.

"No, these poor slobs aren't," Rattus answered, misunderstanding. "They're the kindest, sweetest rats you ever saw. They have to be—they've all got the good professor's little doodad in their brains."

"All of them?" Miranda was shocked.

"All of them—except me. It's my turn tonight. Or it would've been. . . . Say, listen, do you think you could give me a hitch to the first floor. There's a nifty little hole in one of the rooms there. It'll let me get to my pals to tell them what's been going on here. Then we can mobilize. . . ."

"You cannot go back to the sewer. There is no time," Naja said, emerging from under Miranda's sweater.

"My mother's snout!" Rattus leaped across the counter as far away from Naja as he could and stared at her, at a loss for words. Finally, he said, "What is this?" He looked at Miranda. "You're not from some Save Our Furry Friends group after all, are you?"

She shook her head. "We're here to stop Professor N-Chant."

"Okay, let's all go to the sewer. My friends and I can use all the help we can get."

"There is no time," Naja repeated firmly. "We must leave this world immediately."

"Oh. Well, then, it's been nice knowing you. Now if I could just hitch that ride . . ."

"You must leave with us," said Naja, and she told him why.

The rat cocked his head and listened. "The Correct Combination, huh? Name has a nice ring to it. And you say I'm a member?"

"Yes—and now we must reach the basket."

"The basket?"

"It is what takes us from world to world. We must go to it at once. Miranda will give you a ride in her pocket— will you not, Miranda?"

"Yes, all right," Miranda agreed with a sigh.

Rattus was even less enthusiastic. "Pocket, huh? Pants pocket?" He eyed the distance between her waist where Naja was wrapped and her hips where the pocket lay.

"I will not harm you," the snake assured.

"Glad to hear it," the rat replied, but didn't move. "And just where is this basket?"

"We hid it outside in a bush," Miranda told him.

"Oh. Outside," the rat said, and his manner seemed to alter slightly. "Well, all right. Let's go get it then." He sidled over to Miranda.

She lifted him up, surprised at how soft and sleek his fur felt. He was a bit plump as well, unlike the general—the one advantage to living in a cage. Gently she helped him into her pocket. It was so deep and her pants so baggy he scarcely made a bulge.

Bastable checked the hall. "All clear," he said.

They left, Miranda once again trying not to appear frantic. Reaching the stairwell easily, they took it down one flight to the lobby. Only a short walk now and they'd be out the front door.

But then a door beside them swung open, and suddenly Rattus scrambled out of Miranda's pocket down to the floor. "Thanks for the lift," he called as he dashed into the room and out of sight.

"Hey!" cried out a man who was coming out of the same room.

Miranda pushed him aside and ran after Rattus, calling his name. But the rat was gone. Patsy P-Body—with her friends—was standing there instead. And in her arms was Naja's basket.

CHAPTER

II

"That's mine," Miranda said, seizing hold of the basket. She had one thought in her head—to get out of the laboratory and down to the sewer where they might find Rattus and make their escape.

Bastable had the same idea. "Get it away from her. Now!" he shouted.

"It's the emo," said one of the girls.

Miranda didn't know the term, but she didn't ask what it meant. Neither did Patsy. She kept her eyes on Miranda, tightened her grip on the basket, and said, "Is it? Why'd you hide it in a bush then?"

Without bothering to ask how she'd happened to find it, Miranda belligerently stated, "None of your business."

"Everything's our business," said the third girl. "We're prefects, and we're taking this to Ms. A-Range." Then she quoted, " 'No personal items larger than a flight bag are to be brought to the laboratory.' "

Prefects! Miranda snorted. She didn't know that word either, but she could guess its definition—finks, snoops, stool pigeons.

"You have the wrong office," a red-haired man spoke up. He was sitting at a table, placidly building a construction of what appeared to be straws. The tense scene seemed to have little effect on him or on his identical twin, sitting opposite, building an identical construction.

More implants, thought Miranda. To her self-disgust, she was grateful. If they were implants, they probably weren't guards.

"Ms. A-Range's office is upstairs," he continued.

Patsy was listening to him, and the shift in her attention weakened her hold on the basket. Taking advantage, Miranda tugged and nearly succeeded in wresting it from her. But Patsy was stronger, and she had help. The two other girls grabbed Miranda's shoulders and pinned back her arms. Patsy grinned at her triumphantly.

But her smile was quickly erased as the basket was suddenly yanked from her arms and spirited to a spot in midair some five feet away from her.

"Hurry up, Miranda!" Bastable shouted, for it was he, unseen by the girls, who now clutched the basket. "Open the door. I can't go through it with this thing."

"Interesting," the red-haired twins said, looking on with identical lackluster smiles.

"She's not an emo—she's a Morphite," said one of the girls, and the others looked terrified.

"Hurry up!" Bastable yelled again. He took a step forward just as a panel by his side slid open and the basket was plucked neatly from his grasp.

"Professor N-Chant!" gasped Patsy.

Bastable lunged and sunk his claws into the man's shoulder once, then again. Though he could not see the fenine, the professor could feel him. He managed easily to grab Bastable by the scruff of the neck. The fenine went limp—and visible.

The girls stared at Bastable in curiosity and alarm.

But the professor smiled pleasantly. "Party tricks?" he asked. Everything about his looks was pleasant and ordinary—except for his bright green eyes.

"Ha ha," the girls laughed, thinking it must be some kind of joke, even if they didn't get it.

"Oh, professor, we admire you so much. You're our idol," one of them babbled.

"I'm flattered." He consulted his watch. "One half hour. There's time," he said to himself, and looked up at Miranda. "I'd like to have a talk with you—you and your friend."

Miranda's mouth opened, but not a word escaped. The man's emerald gaze held her. *He* is *the Charmer*, Miranda told herself. *Naja, do something*. But Naja didn't even stir.

Professor N-Chant dismissed Patsy and her friends and the red-haired twins. For a full minute after they'd gone, he did nothing but smile and stare at Miranda. Then at last he said in a mellifluous voice, "I'm surprised to see your friend here. He is very far from home, isn't he?"

Unable to stop herself, Miranda nodded.

"I shouldn't wonder if you're far from home as well . . ." He paused, leaving a blank space for her to fill in her name.

"Miranda," she obliged.

"Miranda," he repeated. "Well, you two certainly put Ms. A-Range out of commission for a while. I don't know how you managed it."

To her horror, Miranda knew she was about to tell him. *Those eyes*, she thought. *They drag the words right out of you*. "I . . . we . . ." she began.

But then there was a faint scrabbling sound in a corner of the room. Professor N-Chant's eyes flickered toward it—as did Miranda's. Nothing was there, but the spell was broken. Miranda inhaled deeply. When the Charmer looked back at her, she was able to avoid his eyes.

"Where is he?" he demanded. "Where is Rattus?"

"I don't know," Miranda answered truthfully.

"Have you put him in this?" He tapped the basket.

"There's nothing in there."

"We'll see." He opened the lid, peered inside, and frowned. Then he set the basket on the floor and edged it tantalizingly near Miranda with his foot, smiling as he did.

Suddenly Miranda blurted out, "You're turning the beings of this world into zombies!"

The Charmer chuckled. "Ah, you wish to have a philosophical discussion on the merits of my implant? Perhaps another time. . . . Now, where is Rattus?" He advanced toward her with Bastable still in tow. "In your pocket perhaps." He reached out his free hand toward Miranda.

All at once Naja's head thrust out from beneath Miranda's sweater and she struck him, puncturing his wrist deeply with her fangs.

Startled, the Charmer dropped Bastable and clutched his hand.

Her jewel blazing bright as the Charmer's eyes, Naja uncoiled from Miranda's waist and slid down, poised to strike again.

The Charmer stepped back, a tremor passing over his

face. But just as quickly it was gone, and he was smiling again. "So there is another," he said. "I should have known. The more the merrier, eh?" he snickered.

Miranda trembled. The man did not show any signs of imminent collapse. In fact, he looked stronger, as though the knowledge he'd just acquired was an antidote to Naja's venom and an elixir, all rolled into one.

Bastable woozily tried to rise. The Charmer kicked him lightly in the neck and down he went again. "You want philosophy, Miranda," he said with what was almost affection. "I'll give you some. With this simple device"— he pulled a small filament from his pocket—"we can eliminate fear and anger. We can end murder, crime, war. This we can do, and more. And this is what you and your friends want to destroy."

"Do not listen to him, Miranda," said Naja. "There is no lasting peace when some are slaves and others masters."

"If the slaves do not know they are slaves, then slavery does not exist," the Charmer argued back. He looked again at Miranda. "Your friend is leading you astray. Ask her if *her* world is free of slaves."

"It is. I saw it," Miranda cried.

"Did you? Or did you see what she wanted you to see?"

Miranda blinked. Suddenly her mind was a jumble. What was the truth? What had she seen?

"Do not listen to him," Naja hissed. "Do not look at him. He will hypnotize you."

The Charmer laughed. "And what does she call the

thing she did to you? Let her return to her miserable world, Miranda. Stay here. Join us. Your fenine friend can stay as well, and of course, the little rat. . . ."

Miranda rubbed her forehead, which was beginning to throb, and found herself moving slowly toward him, lifting her face to those green eyes.

But a sudden movement distracted her. Behind the Charmer, a blur of brown fur popped out of a hole in the floor.

"Rattus!" she cried, without thinking.

The Charmer whirled around and lunged at the rat, who made no move to escape.

"Quick, into the basket!" Rattus shouted at Miranda, Naja, and Bastable as the Charmer's hands closed around him.

Naja obeyed at once. Miranda grabbed Bastable and shoved him inside, but hesitated to get in herself.

Clutching Rattus, the Charmer turned his gaze on her again.

"Now!" the rat shouted.

Miranda thought he was yelling at her. But she was wrong. He was issuing a command to a different party. He was summoning the rat army, which, with one gigantic thrust, pushed up the floorboard, poured into the room, and swarmed over the Charmer.

He tore at the rodents, pummeling, crushing. Miranda let out a cry, which was stifled by Rattus, who had broken free of his grasp and was streaking toward the basket.

With rats clinging to his arms and legs, the Charmer made a grab for him. He might have caught Rattus if

Miranda had not scooped him up instead and leaped into the basket.

The door crashed open and two burly guards ran in. But they were too late. The last thing Miranda saw as she closed the lid were the Charmer's furious green eyes. *Next time we meet*, they vowed, *you and your friends will be mine.*

CHAPTER
12

"Weird."

"You'll get used to it, rat. We did."

"You did what?"

"Got used to this conveyance." Bastable pointed at the basket, resting at their feet.

"I'm not talking about the basket. I'm talking about all this . . . leafy stuff." Rattus replied, staring at the surrounding landscape.

"What's the matter? Haven't you ever seen grass and trees before?"

"Sure, but not in such . . . quantity."

"You call this quantity? Why, in Appledura there are forests so vast you could enter one in summer and greet winter when you leave. This forest is nothing. It stops nearly where it starts."

"It was bigger once," said Naja with such gravity that both Rattus and Bastable turned to her. "Much bigger. The trees say so."

"It still seems plenty big to me," said Rattus after a pause. "A human could stay well hidden here for a while—not to mention a rat. Or, if what you told me is true, somebody like the Charmer."

"He is not in this forest."

"Are you sure?"

"I am sure."

"Are you also sure that we're in the right place?" asked

Bastable with deference. He had no wish to antagonize the serpent. "You didn't go into your trance."

"I did—in the basket. It was not full shukor, but it told me where we had to go."

"Did it also tell you whom we're looking for here?"

"Yes, in part. A being named Bennu and some kind of a dog."

"A dog!" snarled Bastable.

"You'll get used to it, Your Highness," said Rattus with great innocence.

The fenine bestowed upon the rodent his most regally withering look, which Rattus ignored. "So," he went on, "where are these characters?" He looked up at the sky, which was showing signs of approaching sunset. "Do we go looking for them right away, or do we find some place to hole up for the night? Let's take a vote. I vote Hole Up. How about you, Miranda? Miranda?"

Miranda didn't answer him. At the moment she was not thinking about where to spend the night, nor even where they were. Her attention was fixed on a single— and singularly—tall tree, or more precisely on the scores of fat, orange globes dangling from its high branches. Mouth watering, belly burbling, she stared up at them and thought that if at that moment the Charmer came along and offered her one of the fruits in exchange for her soul, she'd probably accept.

Rattus followed her gaze. "Hmmm," he said. "Those look tasty. Why don't you grab a few?"

"I won't be able to reach them," she answered, hearing him at last.

"You mean you can't climb the tree?"

"I can climb it, I think—I'm a good climber—but I can't get out on those narrow branches."

"No problem," assured Rattus. He scrambled up her side and into her pocket. "You do the major leg work. I'll take care of the rest."

He sounded so confident that, for the first time in a while, Miranda smiled. Then she began to climb the tree. It wasn't as easy as she'd hoped, for although the trunk was knobbly and there were plenty of toeholds, she was rather tired and more than a little weak from her recent narrow escape. Still, she managed at last to hoist herself into the fork.

"Okay," said Rattus, clambering out onto a limb. "How many do you want?"

"Half a dozen should last us awhile," Miranda said, nearly drooling.

"You got it." Nimbly, the rat picked his way across the big branch to a thinner one at the tip of which the fruit drooped heavily. With several quick snips, he bit through the stems. The orange globes thudded softly to the leaf litter on the ground below. Then he nimbly returned to Miranda, but he didn't go straight into her pocket. "While we're up here, we might as well see what's out there," he explained. "You know, check out the lay of the land."

Miranda was so hungry she didn't care if the lay of the land included a volcano about to erupt. But when Rattus teasingly said, "That is, if you're not about to faint from hunger," she harrumphed that she'd never fainted in her life and wasn't about to do so now.

Together they peered out at the vista. They saw that the woods ended abruptly, the ragged edge running right into fields of lush plants flowering scarlet and yellow. Towering beyond the fields like a solitary witness was a high, forbidding mountain, lavender gray in the fading sunlight. The sight of the mountain made Miranda shiver. But the fields were pleasantly, soothingly familiar. "Farms," she said.

Though Rattus had never seen any, he knew what the word meant. "The people must have stopped working for the evening and gone inside to those houses."

Miranda took in the tumbledown shacks at the perimeter of the fields and was both dismayed and surprised by their contrast to the gay and orderly rows of plants. "They must be poor," she said.

"Why?"

"Their homes are in pretty bad shape."

The houses looked fine enough to Rattus, for whom all buildings were equal so long as they kept the rain off his back. But, willing to take a human's word about the condition of another human's home, he said, "Maybe they don't care about their houses. Maybe they spend all their time on their ..." he fumbled for the right word, "... crops."

"Maybe," Miranda said doubtfully. Then she added, "I wonder what they're growing."

"I don't know—but they've sure got a lot of it."

Miranda gave a little laugh, and her belly answered with a great gurgle.

"Suppertime," said Rattus, climbing into her pocket.

She smiled, and couldn't resist patting her hip just over the bulge of Rattus's small, round body.

The fruit was delicious, but not substantial enough. An hour later, when the group had settled down for the night in a sheltered grove of overhanging bushes, Miranda was ravenous again. She tried to tell herself that Robin Hood and his Merry Men probably spent many a hungry night in Sherwood Forest, but it didn't much help. She wasn't used to going to bed without a sizable dinner.

Bastable, who'd gone off earlier and caught his own supper, which Miranda did not care to hear about, suggested that in the morning they go to one of the farms Miranda and Rattus had spotted. "You can always get something to eat on a farm. I have visited many in Appledura. No fenine ever refused me a bowl of milk, a few fresh eggs, a piece of cheese, or a fresh handful of catnip. Farmers are very generous."

Sitting on Miranda's knee, Rattus gave a rattish snort. "Did it ever occur to you, Your Highness, that their generosity might have had something to do with your title?" he said.

"What do you mean?"

"I mean, if you weren't their king, they wouldn't have given you diddly squat."

"That's where you are wrong. I did not go to them as a monarch, but in peasant garb," Bastable declaimed triumphantly.

"Really? I bet that sure fooled 'em," Rattus said with a dry sarcasm not lost on the fenine. "Why don't you try that here and see what you get?"

"Why don't you? That's one reception I'd like to see."

"Stop it, both of you!" ordered Miranda. "I'm tired of your bickering. I'm tired, period."

"Miranda is right. If we do not learn peace among ourselves, the Charmer will defeat us without lifting a finger," said Naja.

There was a long and grudging silence. Then at last Rattus said, "Why are you here, Bastable? What has this Charmer done to you and your precious . . . your Appledura."

"You don't care to know, rat . . . Rattus."

"Yes, he does," said Naja. "Tell him, King Bastable."

"No."

Suddenly Miranda was wide awake. "Then tell me. I want to know. I deserve to know. I'm here because of you, sort of, and besides, I'm your friend. Tell me about the Charmer. Tell me about Snare."

Bastable looked up at the sky. The moon was rising. It looked much like the Earth's moon, a nearly full yellow sphere. Bastable thought of Appledura's twin blue orbs and grew homesick. "Snare," he rasped. "Snare was . . . Snare came . . ." He stopped, rubbed his face, then began again in the softer voice of someone with a long and painful tale to tell. "When I was a very young princeling, there were difficult times in Appledura. A blight fell upon the waters, a drought fell upon the land. The fish disappeared, the grass withered, the mice died. We were all hungry—even my father and mother, the king and queen. No one could help us. No one except Snare.

"He was a fenine, like the rest of us, except his eyes were a deeper, shinier green, the color of verdifish.

Where he came from we never knew. One day he simply appeared at court. He seemed a cheerful being, and that in itself was surprising as we were all too hungry to feel very happy. But Snare was jolly and entertaining. He told fascinating stories. He did magic tricks. My parents liked him. Everyone liked him. Except me. And I could not say why. Except that he seemed to be . . . everywhere.

"One day Snare said he knew another kind of magic —real magic—and that he could make the fish return to the waters if we did what he asked. . . ." Bastable paused, once again rubbing his face.

"What did he ask?" asked Miranda.

"A most peculiar thing. He said that every Appledurian was to send him a tuft of tail fur."

"What did he want that for?" Rattus queried, becoming drawn in, partly against his wish, to the story.

"He said it would insure our good faith in him. Well, although my fellow fenines liked Snare, they had little reason as yet to believe he could make our fish return. But we were so hungry and the request seemed so harmless that Appledura did what he asked."

"Then what happened?" said Miranda.

"The fish began to reappear—in twice the numbers as before the blight. Rain came, and with it new growth, many mice. Soon we were well fed again, and Appledura was convinced it was Snare's doing. He was showered with gifts, treasures, all of which he declined.

" 'You have already given me what I have requested. I trust that should you need me again, you will grant then too what I shall ask.' With that, he left.

"Years passed. My father died and I succeeded to the throne. I had a happy reign. Appledura was rich and prosperous. Until once again the fish began to disappear; the seas, the lakes, and rivers dried; the crops failed. Those old enough to remember the last famine began to talk among themselves, and what they murmured was Snare's name. It was not long before he came, as he had before. Once again he promised to work his wiles in exchange for another request. The last had been so simple, so innocent my fenines had no fear that this second would be no worse. They were wrong. For this time Snare asked that each family tell him its ancestral name."

Naja let out a sudden hiss. It made Miranda and Rattus jump.

"I don't get it," said the rodent when he settled down. "What's in a name?"

When Bastable did not immediately reply, Naja said, "In my land to reveal one's ancestral name is to give away one's soul."

Bastable cleared his throat with a growl. "We Appledurians wouldn't put it quite the same way. We would say if you tell someone your ancestral name, that someone becomes one of two things to you—your friend for life or your Master."

"And Snare became the latter," said Rattus.

"Did everyone give in to him?" asked Miranda, already knowing the answer.

"Everyone but me."

"And for that he threw you out of Appledura."

A low and mournful sound escaped the fenine. "It was

not Snare who forced me to leave my world, but my own fenines, slaves to their new lord, King Snare."

Naja hissed again. Miranda inhaled sharply, tears of rage springing to her eyes. Even Rattus was momentarily struck dumb by the injustice.

There was a long silence. Then Bastable said, "Now you know why I am here, Miranda. You must forgive me for not having told this sorry tale sooner. It brings me grief and shame to tell it now."

"Why should you be ashamed?" she asked softly. "You did nothing wrong."

"Nor did I do anything right. I could not feed my fenines. I could not keep Snare away. I could not stop him from"—he looked at where Naja lay coiled, barely making her out in the dark—"taking their souls."

But it was Rattus who spoke instead of the snake. His determined voice pierced the darkness that shrouded them all. "You'll stop him yet, Bastable," he said. "We'll *all* stop him yet."

CHAPTER
13

Miranda opened her eyes with a start. Someone was staring down at her—a face the color of ginger ale, long and very straight black hair, and large, dark, teardrop-shaped eyes. She gasped and tried to rise. The stranger gabbled something hoarsely and pulled out a knife. She froze. A sentence flashed through her head, one letter at a time, like type on a computer screen: "T-o-o b-a-d I'-m g-o-i-n-g t-o m-i-s-s m-y t-h-i-r-t-e-e-n-t-h b-i-r-t-h-d-a-y."

But the stranger stood there, unmoving. Miranda realized he was only a boy, not many years older than herself, and he looked as frightened as she.

"We will bow to the people's wishes," Bastable's fuzzy voice cut through the tense silence. Miranda glanced at him out of the corner of her eye. He was sound asleep. So were Naja, buried under layers of leaves, and Rattus. Miranda prayed the boy would not notice the rat, curled near her side. She suspected that rats were as little appreciated in this world as in hers.

Suddenly, from beyond the bushes, there was a low whistle. The boy twitched, then whistled back. Then, hoisting a large sack in one hand, he spit out something at Miranda before running away.

For another minute, Miranda didn't move. Then she scrambled to her knees and urgently whispered, "Bastable, Rattus, Naja, wake up. Hurry."

The fenine and the rodent woke immediately, but Miranda had to brush the leaves off the snake and warm her with her hands to rouse her.

"What's the matter?" asked Rattus. "What's going on?"

"A boy with a knife. Here," Miranda replied. She could still see his face, although in a detached way—as if what had just happened hadn't happened to her, but to someone else.

"Where did he go?" Bastable sprang to his feet, ready to hunt down the interloper.

"Let him be," warned Miranda, aware of but not understanding an odd trace of protectiveness in her tone. The boy had a knife. He could be a dangerous enemy. He could be one of the Charmer's disciples, who and whatever they were in this strange world. "Let's just get out of here."

"Where do you wish to go?" asked Naja.

"You tell me," Miranda snapped. When Naja did not reply, she said, in a less harsh voice, "The farms. At least we'll be able to see who we're dealing with there. There aren't so many hiding places. And I'll—we'll—be able to get something to eat—if they don't shoot me on sight, that is."

"I do not feel you are in danger of being shot," said Naja. She did not mention what other type of danger Miranda might be in.

"I'm going to stick out a mile. I mean, judging from what that boy looked like, there's no way I'll be taken for a native. I can't even speak the language here."

"I cannot change your appearance, but I can help with your speech—if you will permit it."

"I'll permit it."

Naja touched her jewel to Miranda's forehead. "Now you will be able to speak and understand the words spoken here."

Miranda felt a familiar ping, but nothing else. Then she asked, "But what about the food? I can't just take something for nothing."

"Why not?" interrupted Bastable. "As I said, farmers are generous. The appearance of a traveler is a diversion for them, especially in a world most likely devoid of TV and that other machine your people are so fond of, the VRC."

"VCR," Miranda corrected. "And I don't think I'd feel right, just being a diversion. I think these people are poor, but I have no money or anything else to give them."

"You have your hands and the sweat of your brow," put in Rattus, who'd managed to hold his tongue during Bastable's remarks.

"What do you mean?"

"I mean, you can offer to work for your meal."

"Work?" Bastable said with intense disdain.

But Miranda looked at Rattus with approval. The rodent was proving very good at practical advice. "Yes," she said. "I think that might do."

A short time later, with Naja around her waist, Rattus in her pocket, Bastable by her side, and the basket in her arms, she was walking out of the forest into the fields.

The dense rows of plants towered over her head, and the flowers gave off a distinct musky perfume that made Rattus sneeze. At first Miranda found it somewhat over-powering as well, but she grew more and more used to it until she actually began to like the aroma.

In the middle of the field, she set down the basket, plucked a flower, sniffed it, and then, without knowing why, rubbed it against her lips and cheeks.

"Come on, Miranda," urged Bastable. "I thought you were hungry." He might as well have added, "I am." The whine in his voice gave him away anyway, making him sound like Miranda's neighbor's cat when it came begging to be fed.

"Hmmm? Oh, yes. Yes, I am," Miranda said dreamily.

Rattus a-chooed again. "Well, get a move on, will you?" he ordered irritably, "before I sneeze off my whiskers."

"All right," agreed Miranda, and she forced herself to take up the basket and walk on.

Finally, she and her companions came out of the field into the dry, dusty front yard of the rickety farmhouse. No one was about as yet. Miranda stood there, blinking, trying to decide what to do. She felt confused and slightly dazed.

"Knock on the door," said Bastable.

"Do you think I should?"

"That's usually the way to rouse people, is it not?"

"Oh, well, yes. But perhaps I should wait." She blinked again. The muzzy feeling was wearing off, but now her eyes were watering and she had a dull headache. *I never get headaches*, she thought. *It must be the lack of food.* She put down the basket again and rubbed her head. She did not think of hiding the thing here—somehow it did not seem a good idea.

Peering around, she noticed that there was a water pump a few feet away. At least she hoped it was for water. Crossing to it, she worked the handle up and down. It squeaked loudly and a clear liquid poured out. She tasted it gingerly. It was water all right. Filling the cup that dangled from the pump, she took a deep draught and offered some to Bastable. He declined. She splashed the water on her face. Then the front door of the house opened.

A man came out. He was short and crabbed and his face, framed by long black hair, seemed sucked-in, as though the skin had no resilience, the bones no firmness. Miranda thought the pump's noise must have roused him. She hoped he wasn't annoyed, or worse. *Naja, I thought you said you would fix it so I could speak here,* she asked silently. *How do I say "Good morning"?* Instantly, the words came into her mind. "Dai-ya," she said aloud. "Dai-ya."

But the man didn't even glance her way. Trembling and twitching, he shambled to a smaller, shedlike building some twenty feet from his house and disappeared inside.

"Friendly," Miranda muttered.

"Perhaps he is deaf," said Bastable.

Miranda looked at him. That idea had never occurred to her, and she was rather surprised it had occurred to the fenine who was not known for his sensitivity.

"How can I communicate with him if he's deaf?" she

murmured, feeling panicky. "Naja, is there a sign language I can use?"

"There may be, but I cannot help you to know it," replied the snake.

"I don't think he's deaf," Rattus said, peering out of Miranda's pocket.

"How do you know that?" asked Bastable.

"Because that's him singing away in there and he's got near-perfect pitch."

"How do you know *that*?" Miranda stared at him in amused disbelief.

"I was born in a melocron factory," he said, as if that explained everything.

Miranda had no time to ask him what a melocron was because just then the man came out of the shed. *It is him, isn't it*, she asked herself, because he scarcely looked like the same person at all. His shoulders were no longer hunched. His hands and legs weren't shaking, and his face was full and calm.

"Dai-ya," she said again, very loudly, and this time he turned to face her.

It took him a while to react, and when he did, brow puckering, lips pursed, he seemed not so much suspicious as a man trying to remember what it meant to feel that way. "Gei qua?" he asked, pronouncing each word slowly. "Who are you?"

With Naja's help, Miranda told him. "I am a . . . stranger here, traveling over the mountains to . . . to . . . bring this gift . . ." she gestured toward the basket, "to a friend." She'd made up the explanation on the spot, and could think of a whole lot of reasons why the man wouldn't believe it.

But oddly enough he did not question her story. He did not seem to have heard it. "I have none to spare," he said. He glanced at the shed and one side of his face twitched.

Miranda gave a puzzled frown. She hadn't yet asked for food and the man was already turning her down. Was he telepathic, like Naja? "I don't require much," she told him, the strange language coming to her naturally now. "A little bread . . . Whatever you can spare."

"I have none to . . ." the man started to repeat, then stopped and stared at Miranda. "Bread." He spoke as if trying to make sense of the word.

"Yes. I have not eaten much in a long time. I am very hungry."

"Bread," the man repeated. "You want bread."

"I am willing to work for it."

"You will work for bread?"

"Yes," Miranda replied, trying not to sound impatient. Perhaps the man was mentally, and not aurally, impaired.

But as he stood there staring at her, the expression stealing over his face belied that. He began to laugh, and Miranda saw that his teeth and tongue were pale blue.

He was still laughing when the door of his house opened again. A woman and three children came out. Twisted and quivering, much as her mate had been, the woman headed straight for the shed with one child in tow. A second, the biggest, followed, slouching at her heels. But the youngest bounced jerkily over to Miranda and began plucking at her sweater like a dog worrying a pile of rags. "Don't!" Miranda said sharply. She did not want Naja to be exposed.

The child let go of the sweater and began slapping Miranda's legs instead. Rattus let out an involuntary and pained squeak when one of the little girl's blows landed across his hidden back. Bastable skipped out of her way to avoid being stepped on. "Stop it! Cut it out!" Miranda shouted. She didn't know whether or not it was bad manners to discipline someone else's child in this land, and she didn't care.

The man, presumably the child's father, took her by the shoulders and pushed her in the direction of the shed. She caromed over and into it. The door shut behind her.

After another interminable pause, the man said, "So. You will work and I will give you *bread*." He emphasized the word and laughed again.

Miranda took a deep breath. "Thank you," she said. "You will not regret it. I am a good worker. I can do many jobs. I can paint the walls, sweep the floors, clean the stove. . . ."

The man shook his head. "There is only one job here," he said. "Only one." He gestured at the field. "Tending the ah-sha."

"Oh, I see," said Miranda, although she didn't. "The ah-sha."

"Yes. Beautiful, is it not? Come." The man led her to the edge of the field. "See how the sun gives its power to the blossoms. Hear how the wind speaks to its leaves. Ahhh-shhhaaa. Ahhh-shhhaaa. Without the ah-sha, we are nothing. Without the ah-sha, we cease to be. It is our life, the ah-sha. Flower of heaven. Essence of the gods."

Miranda gazed at the plants, oddly mesmerized. As she watched, the dense stalks parted and a young man came into view. He was tall and muscular with a smooth tawny face and black hair to his shoulders. Miranda gasped when she saw him, for it was none other than the boy from the woods.

CHAPTER
14

The boy's jaw clenched and his eyes grew rounder in alarm.

Bastable, who'd heard Miranda gasp, hissed, "Is this the one?"

Miranda didn't answer him. She was still staring at the boy. His eyes shifted subtly toward the man, who appeared to be his father, and then back to Miranda. *Don't say anything*, his gaze pleaded. *Don't tell him you've seen me before.*

"I can disarm him. The knife will come in handy." Bastable started forward.

Miranda's hand snapped out and she seized the fenine's tail. Her arm vibrated slightly with Bastable's brief struggle to break free, then relaxed.

The boy, who saw the gesture but not its purpose, tensed further. His father did not see it at all. Realizing that the boy thought she was making a hostile motion at him, Miranda opened her hand and held it out placatingly. "Dai-ya," she said.

Surprise flickered over the boy's face, but he quickly composed himself. "Dai-ya," he responded in a deep voice.

"You are up early," the man said to him, and his face transformed again, taking on a decidedly doltish look.

"I was catching pingkei," he said thickly. He reached

toward the nearest stalk, plucked off a beetlelike bug, and crushed it between his broad thumb and forefinger.

"That's good, son." His father nodded.

"Early is the best time to catch pingkei," the boy went on and then laughed, "Hyuh-hyuh." He made no mention of the woods or the sack Miranda had seen him carrying there.

The rest of his family came out of the shed then. The children were calm now. Their mother was no longer quivering. They all looked at Miranda with only vague interest.

"Dai-ya," she greeted them. "I am Miranda."

"Meeranda," the smallest child repeated. No one else tried to say the word, nor did anybody offer his or her name.

"We'll eat now, then tend the ah-sha," said the father. He started toward the house, the mother and children at his heels.

Miranda glanced sideways at the boy. He was looking back at her and his expression was clear and pointed. *I am in your debt*, it said, *and I don't like it one bit.*

Miranda was hot. So hot that the top of her head felt like the bottom of a frying pan. So hot that even her fingernails seemed to be sweating. She stooped down to poke the six hundred and sixth (or was it six hundred and eighth) hole in the soil and lay into it the six hundred and sixth (or six hundred and eighth) flat, oval seed. Three fat drops of perspiration watered her work. Wiping her face on the sleeve of her shirt (she'd shed her sweater hours ago), she prayed that lunchtime would come soon.

"This is the most inefficient method of planting I've ever seen," said Bastable, ambling beside her up the row. "In Appledura we have something called a *dibbledabble*. It will dig holes and spit seeds into each one faster than you can say its name."

Miranda felt like hurling a stinging retort at him. She was sure Rattus would have produced a terrific one—but Rattus was not in Miranda's pocket. Without being seen, she'd let him out near the house where he could scrounge for some food and for some information. Naja was also somewhere in—or more likely under—the house, trying to keep cool and to guard the basket, although Miranda suspected it did not need much guarding. She wished Bastable had joined the others, but he'd insisted on sticking with her in case she needed help. Some help he'd been. All morning long he'd done nothing but complain —while Miranda did all the work.

And what work. First she'd had to follow behind a plow in a newly tilled field to pick up any large, obstructive stones. The plow was drawn by a broad-shouldered, stolid animal called a *moomak*. Miranda thought it looked like it was part horse, part ox, and part armored truck. Miranda tried to communicate with the moomak, murmuring in the animal's great ear when no one was looking, but with no success. *You've gotten so used to talking animals you're surprised when one of them can't hold a conversation*, she told herself and nearly laughed. Since she'd just filled her belly at last and the sun wasn't yet scorching the fields, she still had a sense of humor.

But her sense of humor was now long gone. After ridding the field of stones, she had had to dump and rake in fertilizer from a barrow. Then, as the sun rose high in the sky, the planting began. Now, during the most sweltering part of the day, it was still going on. As was Bastable.

"And what a ridiculous time of day to be working in the fields. Haven't these people ever heard of a midday nap? I'm roasting out here."

Miranda could take it no longer. "Why don't *you* go take a nap, King Bastable?" she burst out.

Bastable gave her a hurt look and, without another word, stalked away toward the house.

The boy, who was the nearest to Miranda, turned and stared at her, confused by her outburst at the invisible fenine.

Refusing to look back at him, she bent to plant another seed. Suddenly, a wave of dizziness overcame her and she sat heavily on the ground. When she looked up, the boy was standing over her. His father had gone to a neighboring farm to get some heat cones to shield the developing plants and left him in charge. He handed her a canteen. "Take a drink," he offered in his slow, lazy voice. But Miranda saw a sharp command in his eyes.

She accepted the canteen, took a long swallow from it, and gave it back. The boy hooked it to his belt. Then he took off his broad-brimmed hat made of some kind of straw. "Wear this," he said. "It will keep off the sun."

"But then *your* head will be bare," Miranda replied.

"Don't worry about my head. It is used to the sun."

Miranda studied him briefly. His light tunic was soaked with sweat, but he showed no other signs of being bothered by the heat. "All right," she agreed, taking the hat from him with gratitude. The straw was soft and pliable, like her father's favorite panama. "Nice," she said. "Who made it?"

The boy shrugged, uninterested. "I don't know," he said and turned to go back to his work. Suddenly, his spine stiffened. Turning back to Miranda, he pulled the hat as far down as it would go. His movements were unhurried, but under his breath he hissed, "Keep your head low and say nothing." With a smooth movement, he spun around and began to plant the row next to hers.

Miranda did as he said, and so she did not see the dozen men ride up to the field. In fact, she barely heard their approach, so silent were the two-legged, ostrichlike creatures they rode. But their voices rang out loud and clear enough.

"We are looking for Ten-ree. Have you seen him?" asked their leader.

"Ten-ree? Isn't he gone?" Miranda heard the boy's sluggish reply.

"He's gone, all right. Gone to join the outlaws."

"Outlaws? What outlaws?"

"What outlaws! Why, the ones in those woods."

"Benave-seeking scum!" added the second-in-command. The men laughed.

"There are outlaws in the woods?" said the boy. The men laughed again and the boy joined in, louder than the rest.

Then another person spoke. Though Miranda had not heard her before, she knew at once it was the boy's mother. In a high and brittle voice, she said, "I saw a benave once. It was a long time ago."

There was a sudden silence. It lasted for some time.

The leader broke it at last. "Well, you won't see any these days," he said gruffly. "They're all dead and gone, no matter what the outlaw scum believe."

"That's right." "You can say that again," chorused several voices.

"So if you see Ten-ree before we do—or anyone else, stranger or friend, who may be an outlaw, you can tell him that—and then report him. We catch him and you get a nice reward. Here's a little sample." He tossed something at the boy's feet.

From under her brim, Miranda could not see what it was, only that there was a mad scramble to catch it. She thought the boy had it, but then she heard an excited squeal and saw a small pair of feet race past her toward the house.

"No! Stop! Give me that," the boy called after the figure. Miranda saw him start toward the child.

But the leader stopped him. "Now, now, don't be selfish." He was jocular enough, but behind the jovial tone was an edge of nastiness. "Let the kid have a little fun. She's probably underfoot anyway. They always are at that age. . . . Here, I'm feeling generous today." He threw another small missile to the ground. This time the boy snatched it before anyone else could. "Don't use it all at once—it's high-grade stuff," the leader said. He and his men laughed once more. But this time the boy did not join in. "All right, men, fall out," the leader commanded, and the men moved off. When they were several yards away, he called over his shoulder, "Remember what I said. Turn in an outlaw and you'll find our esteemed prime minister even more generous than I." Then he and his men disappeared into the fields toward the woods.

As soon as they were out of sight, the boy ran after his sister. Dropping the handful of seeds she held into a sack, Miranda tore after him. He did not go into the house, but the shed. Miranda saw him fling open the door and heard his anguished cry before, panting from heat and fear, she reached his side.

There on the bare wooden floor, clutching an empty vial in her small fist, lay the youngest child. Her lips and cheeks were stained bright blue, and she was not breathing at all.

CHAPTER
15

Pushing the boy aside, Miranda knelt beside the little girl. She stared at the prone figure, trying desperately to remember what resuscitation techniques she'd learned in Health class. But she'd spent most of that class imagining she was being rescued from drowning by a handsome young merman and scarcely heard a word her teacher had said. The only thing she could think of now was to tilt the girl's head.

"Breathe into her mouth," a raspy voice told her.

She turned her head. Rattus was peering at her from under a cabinet.

"What? How do you know that?"

"Grew up near the docks—now hurry up. No time to waste. Hold her nose shut and blow." He disappeared.

Pausing only to cast a quick glance at the boy, who was still standing there, smashing one fist into his other palm, too distracted to have heard Rattus, Miranda began to do as the rat had said. *Blow in, take a breath. Blow in, take a breath*, she chanted silently, rhythmically, her mouth sealed tightly around the girl's. Four breaths and she paused. Nothing happened. The child's lungs refused to work. She felt the girl's neck for a pulse. It was there, but faint and stringy. *She's not dead. I won't let her be dead*, Miranda vowed, and began to breathe into her mouth again.

She kept at it, losing track of the time, when suddenly the child gave a cough and a sigh and abruptly opened her eyes.

"Are you all right now?" she asked.

The girl stared blankly at her.

Miranda repeated the question.

The girl's lips curled in a dreamy smile. "Outlaw," she said.

"What? No, I'm not an outlaw. I'm Miranda, remember?"

"Outlaw," the child repeated. Then turning to her side, she curled up and fell into a deep sleep.

Miranda saw a scrap of blanket nearby and covered her with it. When she looked up, the boy was staring at her, a wide range of emotions playing across his face—relief, amazement, and anger.

"You brought her back to life," he said. "Like magic."

"It's called mouth-to-mouth resuscitation. There isn't anything magical about it. You could learn it too. . . . Your sister ought to have a doctor look at her now."

"No doctor will come here. She will be all right now."

Frowning, Miranda bent down and picked up the empty vial. It exuded a familiar musty scent. "Drugs," she realized. "The ah-sha your family grows is made into this. You're all addicts, right? All of you."

When the boy said nothing, she went on, with rising anger, "And for some mouthfuls of bread, I'm helping you support your habit. . . . Your sister, how old is she? Six, seven? Do you care that she uses this stuff? Or are you just annoyed that she didn't leave any of it for you? Go on, say something. Say anything. Or do you also think I'm one of those dangerous outlaws those men were talking about?"

The boy's pale cheeks colored. "I know you are not an outlaw," he said quietly.

"What makes you so sure?"

The boy hesitated briefly, then a look of resolution came into his dark eyes. "Because *I* am," he said.

"You! You are?" Miranda stammered.

In an eloquent, measured voice far different from the oafish one he used with his family and visitors, he said, "Every morning before dawn, I have gone into the forest to bring food and supplies to the men and women hiding there. It was my friend Ten-ree who told me of them. It was he who weaned me from this poison...." He pointed to the vial in Miranda's hand. "And poison it is. It has destroyed my family. It has destroyed my land." His mouth trembled. "This was once a world of great beauty. Forests blanketed it. There were birds and beasts of every description, trees and flowers in abundance. Now the trees and birds and beasts are gone. That patch of woods—and a few other patches here and there—are all that remain of the vast jungles, all cut down to make room for the ah-sha, and only the ah-sha. These woods too shall go—unless the benaves help."

"Who are the benaves?" asked Miranda.

The boy paused, groping for words. "They are birds, but not birds," he said at last. "They are of two worlds —this one we can see and another of the spirit. They help keep harmony between the people and the other spirits, such as Chi-wa of the earth and Chi-na of the sky. They used to fly in the forests until the people began to cut down the trees. Then the benaves left in anger. Most people, including the Long Arms—those soldiers who were here before—think they are dead. But the benaves cannot die. They are immortal. Those in power, especially our prime minister, who introduced the poison and now profit from it, they know, but they lie to the people. However, they cannot fool the outlaws. The outlaws know the benaves exist. They will find them and plead with them to help restore this world."

Caught up in the boy's story and his fervor, Miranda felt a sharp stab of pity. "But those men, they were going to the woods to arrest—or even kill—your friend and the other outlaws."

The boy barked out a short, triumphant laugh. "They will not find him nor any of the others. They left the woods many hours ago for the Silver Mountain. The kamli fever epidemic has ended, the snows have melted, and the passes are open, so they have gone at last. The mountain is where the benaves now dwell, suspended in a dreamless sleep. But we will wake them so our land can live again." The boy's eyes blazed ardently.

"We?" Miranda said.

The boy paused once more, weighing something. Then, looking into Miranda's eyes, he declared with quiet strength, "I go to join them tonight."

Miranda nodded, for she had known that was what the boy would say, and she both understood his decision and feared for his life.

For a moment no other words passed between them. But then the boy said, "Now you hold my secret in your hands. If you choose, you can crush it like a flower. But you did not betray me to my father, and I want to believe you will not betray me now."

"Believe it," said Miranda solemnly. "You can trust me, and I believe I can trust you. You made certain those men would not see that I am a stranger and so ask questions. Now you must have questions too. You must want to know why I'm here."

"Yes," the boy agreed. "I want to know."

"All right. I'll tell you," said Miranda, and she did. As she spoke, the boy's eyes grew wide with disbelief.

"You say you have companions. Who are they? Where are they?" he asked.

"They're . . . around," Miranda said vaguely, glancing toward the cabinet under which Rattus was hiding. "Perhaps you'll meet them later."

The boy frowned. "And you say you do not know who the Charmer is here or what other companions you must find?"

"No. Only that there are two. One is named Bennu and the other is some kind of dog."

The boy's eyebrows disappeared into his long bangs, and he made a small sound of wonder and fear.

"Do you know them, or have you heard of them?" Miranda asked.

He nodded slowly. "Bennu is the empress of the benaves. It is she we seek."

"And the other?"

"The other . . ." The boy smiled strangely. "Allow me to introduce myself. My name is Chao-ji. But my friends call me Iron Dog."

CHAPTER
16

The moomak was grinding its teeth. Not every minute or even every other minute, just often—and loudly—enough to make sure Miranda wouldn't get one wink of sleep. And sleep was what she needed.

"You must rest well and gather all your strength. It is not a long journey, but neither is it an easy one," Iron Dog had said as he led her to the small barn behind the house in which, along with the moomak, lived a flock of drowsy chickenlike birds that laid eggs which came out already hard-cooked. "I will come to the barn at the hour of Terret to wake you."

Miranda did not know when it would be the hour of Terret, but she hoped it was soon. It was bad enough she'd have to climb a mountain at night. But lying awake, listening to a moomak grinding its teeth was even worse.

"Will someone shut that stupid beast up?" Bastable spat churlishly. He'd spent the afternoon sulking in the barn and now he was still sulking, despite the fact that Miranda had apologized earlier for snapping at him.

With a groan, Miranda got up, went over to the massive moomak, and stroked its shaggy head. The animal snuffled her hand briefly and then ignored her. But at least for the time being it stopped grinding its teeth.

Miranda left the creature and made her way over to a wall. She peered through the cracks in the boards, but she couldn't see much besides the dark side of the farmhouse, striped with moonlight. There was no sign yet of Iron Dog. *Iron Dog.* She said the name to herself. *It suits him*, she thought. She'd just met the boy, but already she knew that he was as strong as iron—he had hoisted three heavy sacks of ah-sha seed at one time and carried them on his shoulders as if they were filled with down—and she suspected he was dogged as well. She was glad he would be accompanying them on their journey to find Bennu. He made her feel, if not exactly safe, at least safer.

"Miranda, where are you?" Rattus called lazily from the straw pallet she'd been lying on. The rat had been tucked in the crook of her arm and he missed the warmth.

"Here. Waiting for Iron Dog."

"Well, you can wait here just as well, can't you? Anyway, he'll come when he comes."

"*If* he comes," put in Bastable.

"What do you mean *if*?" Miranda demanded, more heatedly than she'd intended.

"Just what I said, *if* he comes, *if* he keeps his word. I wouldn't trust him or anybody else here."

"You have to trust him," Miranda insisted. "He's one of us."

"How do we know that? How do we know he's really the right 'dog'?"

"You want there to be another dog? I thought you'd be glad the one we've got turned out not to be of the canine variety," said Rattus.

When Bastable ignored him and repeated his allegation, Miranda, fuming, rapped out, "Is he, Naja? Is Iron Dog a member of the Correct Combination?"

The snake, who'd been silent all evening, spoke at last.

"I believe he is," she said. But none of them failed to detect the hint of uncertainty in her voice.

"Ha!" exclaimed Bastable. "She *believes*. But she's not sure. Just like she's never been sure about . . ." He broke off abruptly.

"Me," Miranda finished for him. "Maybe *I'm* the one who's not really part of this group."

"Miranda," Bastable said, regretting his thoughtlessness. "I didn't mean . . ."

But Miranda went on, her voice rising with both hurt and self-doubt. "Maybe when it comes time for the final battle with the Charmer, I'll be useless as a tree stump. Maybe I've just been along for the ride."

"If you were not a member of the Correct Combination, would you have chosen such a ride?" Naja asked quietly. Miranda understood that whatever uncertainty about her the cobra once had was totally gone, and the knowledge soothed and touched her.

After a pause, Rattus said, "Speaking of the Charmer, who and where do you think he is in this place?"

"Do not worry about finding the Charmer in this world, for if we do not find him, he will most certainly find us," said Naja.

"I was afraid you'd say that," Rattus muttered, and the moomak punctuated his comment with a long, rolling belch.

Miranda giggled, but her laughter was brief, for the door cracked open and Iron Dog slid inside and over to the pallet. Cloaked and hooded, he looked more like a shadow than a boy. "Wake up, Miranda. Wake up."

Kneeling down, he felt for her shoulder. Rattus scurried away from his groping hands. "Where are you? For the sake of the Eye of Heaven, where are you?"

"I'm here," she said, coming up behind him. "Is something wrong?"

Iron Dog whirled around with a startled grunt. "I thought we'd have more time," he said, quickly regaining his poise, "but we must leave at once. My mother is gone—and I think she went to summon the Long Arms."

"What? Your mother?" An image came into Miranda's head of the vacant-eyed woman at dinner, lethargically ladling a thick, tasteless gruel into her bowl. Miranda could scarcely believe the woman had the energy or wit to summon anyone. "Why? Why did she go for them?"

"Because of you."

"Me? Your mother also believes I'm an outlaw?"

"She does not know or care what you are. She is interested only in the reward."

"When did she go? How long will it take before they come?"

"I don't know exactly when she left, but it must have been at least three quarters of an hour ago. I have been asleep that long," he said shamefully. "The outpost is behind Chee-sun's farm, two miles from here. The sentinel will need to go another two miles to the station, but by skalim—their mounts—that will take no time at all. So we must go at once. Here, put this on." He handed her a cloak, identical to his own.

Miranda fingered the heavy wool. *It will be too warm*, she thought.

"It will not feel too warm on Silver Mountain," Iron Dog said, hearing her unspoken words. "And it will hide you from the moonlight and the Long Arms' sharp eyes. Quickly now, while I make certain they have not yet arrived." He hurried away.

Naja and Rattus wasted no time in taking their familiar places around Miranda's waist and in her pocket. Then she slipped on the heavy cloak, scooped up the basket, and, with Bastable following, left the barn.

Iron Dog stood a few feet away staring into the darkness.

"Can we go?" Miranda whispered.

"Yes," he replied. Then he saw the basket. "Leave that here. You cannot climb Silver Mountain with that bulky thing."

"I can't leave it. I told you—it is our transportation."

"For you and your companions, wherever they are," said Iron Dog. From his tone, Miranda realized with a start that he had not believed her story after all. Or he had not understood it. Yet, for reasons of his own, he was still willing to take her with him to find Bennu.

"My companions are . . . they will be with us when we . . . reach the mountain. And as for the basket, perhaps . . . perhaps I could . . . um . . . strap it to my back?"

It was too dark for Miranda to see Iron Dog's frown, but she could hear him sigh. "My back is broader," he said. "Wait here." He went back into the barn and came out swiftly with several lengths of rope. One he stuffed in his pack; with the other, he and Miranda tied the basket over the small pack he carried. Then they set out through a scrubby path that cut through a meadow to a spine of low, barren hills.

From the crest of the first, they could see the ah-sha fields, motionless in the still air.

Then Iron Dog said, "Look!"

And as Miranda watched, a row of plants parted to reveal three tall and silent skalim bearing four figures. They dismounted. Three of the figures strode to the barn while the fourth and smallest hovered near the house.

The Long Arms flung open the barn door and ran inside. A few moments later, they came out, cursing and swearing at the cowering figure that was Iron Dog's mother. One smacked her and she fell in a heap to the ground.

"I've seen enough," said Iron Dog. His voice was flat, but his body was shaking.

"So have I," murmured Miranda.

They started across the second hill.

CHAPTER
17

"The air is harder to breathe here," Iron Dog said, pillowing his head on his pack. "But you will become accustomed to it."

The moon had gone down. It was quite dark, although Miranda could see a softening of the sky, as if it were a cocoon about to open and reveal the new day inside. She gathered her cloak more tightly around herself, glad for its warmth—just as Iron Dog said she'd be—and huddled under the overhang he'd found. She couldn't lie down for fear of crushing Naja, so she propped herself up against the rocky wall. They had not gone very far up the mountain, but it had taken them many hours to get where they were, and Iron Dog declared that they now must rest. Miranda knew his insistence had to do with her; she was certain if he'd been alone he would not have stopped at all. But she wasn't about to argue with him. Her legs ached, her chest was tight, and her brain felt like it was floating loosely in her skull.

"What's he talking about?" groused Bastable. Throughout the trip he'd tried to keep his comments to a minimum, but he still did not like Iron Dog and he couldn't say why. He didn't hate him as he did Snare or feel natural enmity as he did toward Rattus. It would never occur to him that what he really felt was jealousy.

"Does he think the air here is good for his nostrils alone?" he sniped now.

"The air *is* harder to breathe here—less oxygen," Miranda replied, both to Bastable and Iron Dog.

"What is oxygen?" they both asked simultaneously.

"It's one of the elements in air—the one we need to breathe. Our lungs take in oxygen and give out carbon dioxide," she explained, thinking she sounded awfully like her old fourth-grade teacher, Ms. Meadows.

It was obvious that neither Bastable nor Iron Dog understood her explanation at all—although Bastable pretended to.

"Ah, yes," he said, "the lungs."

Iron Dog, on the other hand, said, "The air has elements, but I have never heard of this ox-y-gen being one of them. Here we say the air is different on the mountain because it is less lively."

"Less lively," Bastable snorted. "What is he talking about? I feel no difference between the air up here and the air down there."

"Less lively," said Miranda. "I like that. Tell me more about what the people here say."

"About what?"

"About anything. About this mountain."

"It's a magic mountain. That is why Dee Lu Shen has not plundered it."

"Who is Dee Lu Shen?"

"Our beloved prime minister—and the owner of most of the ah-sha factories."

Miranda paused. Then she asked, "Is there silver in this mountain?"

"Silver and mercabar, a metal used in distilling the ah-sha." Iron Dog gave a harsh laugh. "All conversation about my land returns to that poison." He shivered. "Tell me about your land. Do the people there poison themselves too?"

"Some of them do," Miranda answered thoughtfully, "and in a lot of different ways. But many don't—or at least they try not to."

"Is your land pretty? Are there forests and rivers and mountains?"

"Yes. Many of the forests are in danger of being cut down and the rivers of being polluted. But still it is pretty. Where I live there are nice houses and parks and a big lake. When I was younger my mom and dad used to take me boating. I'd pretend we were a family of pirates. . . ." She broke off. The memory—sharp, clear, and sweet—made her suddenly and achingly sad.

"You miss them, don't you?" said Iron Dog. His voice was gentle and compassionate, but it also bore a trace of envy.

"Yes, I do. I didn't think about them much when I was there. I guess I kind of took them for granted. But now I miss them."

"You miss what you had. I miss what I never had," Iron Dog said with bitterness.

It took Miranda aback. There were a few kids in her school who'd been hurt by their parents or other people they relied on. But no one she knew had been hurt by an entire world. She did not know how to comfort the boy. She knew he had to be very strong inside as well as out because, damaged as he was, he still had hope. Impulsively, she reached for his hand.

At first he flinched and she thought he'd pull away. But slowly his fingers closed over hers.

"Maybe you will have it yet," she said quietly, "when we defeat the Charmer."

Iron Dog did not respond immediately. He liked and trusted Miranda more than he liked anyone, except perhaps his friend Ten-ree. He could not explain why this was so—only that it was. She was seeking Bennu. So was he. Good enough. They would seek her together, he reasoned. But he still did not understand this business of a Charmer who traveled from place to place, changing form in each one. He could not believe Miranda was pursuing this being in that funny basket now lying at his feet. And not only Miranda, but her companions as well, whom he had not yet met.

He let go of her hand. "So," he said. "You claim your friends will meet us here on the mountain. When will they join us? How will they know where to find us?"

"Yes, Miranda," Bastable said suddenly and peevishly. "When *will* we join you?"

"Well, uh ..." she stammered. "Well ..." In her head she heard Naja say, "Tell him, Miranda. The time is right." In her pocket, Rattus encouragingly patted her leg. "Well, you see, they ... uh ... they already know where we are," she stuttered.

"They do? How?"

"Because ... because ..."

"Oh, for King Mastermain's sake," Bastable rapped out, springing up and over to Iron Dog. "Because we are already here."

The boy let out a startled cry as the chest-high, furry, bewhiskered creature appeared before him. Scrambling backward, he struck his head on the rocky wall. "Oww ... what ... who ..."

"I am His Majesty, Bastable the Fourth, King of the Fenines, Protector of the Shining Order, member of the Correct Combination. Until now, I have been invisible to you. For many months, I have been Miranda's companion, and if you bring her to any harm, you will answer to me!" He flashed his nails gaudily, unaware that Iron Dog could not see them in the pale rays of light seeping from the sky.

"For *heaven's* sake, Bastable, that's enough!" Miranda snapped, annoyed and embarrassed. "The last thing Iron Dog wants to do is hurt any of us."

If asked, Iron Dog, whose hand was on the hilt of his knife, might not have sworn that was so. Trying to regain his equanimity, he said levelly to Miranda, "The others, are they all like ... that?"

"That!" Bastable spat out. Did none of these louts have any respect? "I told you, I am ..."

Miranda overrode him. "No. The others aren't fenines," she said, reaching into her pocket and cautiously holding out her hand. "This is Rattus."

Iron Dog squinted down. "A guapa?" he said in disbelief. "A common guapa?"

"A guapa," agreed Rattus. "But not common."

"By my moomak's teeth!" Iron Dog exclaimed, this time more in amusement than fear.

"And this," said Miranda, opening her cloak and lifting her sweater, "is Naja."

The cobra slithered down her leg. Rising sinuously in front of him, she said, "I greet you, Iron Dog." She inclined her head, the jewel in her forehead glowing softly.

Clutching his knife, Iron Dog did not make a sound.

"You have no cause to fear me," the snake soothed. "Together we will find the Moon Caves and the Cleft of Sirtis."

Iron Dog's mouth opened. "The Moon Caves? The Cleft of Sirtis?" he whispered hoarsely. "What are they?"

"That is where we will find Bennu—if the Charmer does not find her first."

"The Charmer. We still don't know what face he'll be wearing here," said Rattus.

"Except that whatever one it is, it will have green eyes," said Miranda.

"Green eyes. No one in this land has green eyes. Except for one man. I saw him up close only once, when I was small. He visited our farm," said Iron Dog. "It was before the ah-sha. I sat on his knee."

"Who is he?"

"Our prime minister, Dee Lu Shen. But he has not left his mansion in several years."

"He will leave it now," said Naja.

"Will we meet him? Will we have to fight him here?" Miranda asked, remembering that last look the Charmer had given her in the laboratory.

"Will we—with Bennu—destroy him here, once and for all?" added Bastable, forgetting his vexation as he recalled the purpose of their mission. "Is this where the final battle will be?"

"It will be the final battle for someone," replied Naja.

CHAPTER
18

On a branch of a sturdy evergreen tree by a stream that flowed from the heart of Silver Mountain, a bird was singing. Its song wasn't as musical as a wren's or a house finch's, but Miranda thought it was the sweetest song she'd ever heard. For a few moments it made her forget her sore body. All day they'd been climbing, resting, and climbing some more, slowly making their way toward the mountain's peak. The lower slopes were not that difficult, except for a few patches of scree here and there where it was easy to stumble. But Miranda was unused to and ill-equipped for climbing. She had no boots, no gloves, no thick socks. Iron Dog had padded her sneakers with leaves, cut her a thick walking stick, shared the food and water in his pack—all without a word of complaint, even through Bastable's hectoring about how things were done in Appledura. Miranda could only hope there would be some way she could repay his kindness.

Thinking it would be pleasant to soak her sore feet, she limped over to the cold stream, where Iron Dog stood listening to the bird. "Pretty, isn't it?" she murmured.

He didn't hear her. To him, the song was more than pretty. It was miraculous. He could not recall the last time he'd seen a bird. He knew them only from the books Ten-ree had shown him, volumes no one else cared to read anymore—if one bothered to read anything. His face turned from Miranda and the others so they would not see the tears in his eyes, Iron Dog stared at the singer, murmuring over and over in wonder, "A bird. A bird. A bird."

"A bird," agreed Bastable, in a very different tone.

Miranda turned sharply toward him, taking in his flattened ears and narrowed, gleaming eyes. "Don't you dare. Don't even think of it."

Bastable relaxed with a frown. Plucking at his whiskers, he said, "Well, it isn't Bennu, is it?"

"No," answered Naja seriously. "It is not."

"Then why are you—and *he*"—he nodded contemptuously at Iron Dog—"making a fuss?"

Miranda sighed. "When the fish and mice were mostly gone from Appledura, didn't you get excited if you were lucky enough to find one?"

"Yes, but that was because I was starving."

"Well, Iron Dog is starving too, though not for food."

"I do not understand," said Bastable.

Miranda sighed again. She understood what Iron Dog was feeling, but even she could not feel it as deeply—nor convey it. "Never mind," she said. "Just leave the bird alone." Taking off her sneakers and socks, she plunged her throbbing feet into the icy stream.

"No rats, no birds. What do you expect me to eat around here?" Bastable grumbled.

"These are pretty good," Rattus suggested. He was munching on a fat, kidney-shaped nut. "Have one."

"No, thank you," sniffed Bastable. He turned to Naja, who was sunning herself on a rock. "When will we find

Bennu? We have been traveling all day, and there's been no sign of anyone else."

Suddenly Rattus said, "Now that's a strange bird song if I ever heard one—not that I've heard many."

Miranda listened. From somewhere on the other side of the water, a thin, high piping spiraled upward.

Iron Dog heard it too, and he spun around. "That's no bird. That's a flute. Ten-ree's flute!" he exclaimed. He grabbed Miranda's hand and began to pull her toward the sound.

"Wait," she said, tugging back.

"Yeah, wait for us," agreed Rattus.

Iron Dog stopped. "Sorry," he said to the rat. "I thought perhaps you'd rather stay here."

"You mean *you'd* rather we stay here," said Bastable angrily.

"No ... well, yes. How can I explain you to my friends?"

"Varlet, you need us more than we need you and much more than we need your rebellious friends."

"You will not have to explain us," Naja said. "We will hide from them as we hid from you—until we find Bennu."

"Yes," said Miranda, pulling on her sneakers. "But how are you going to explain me?"

"I have thought about that," said Iron Dog. "I will tell them you are a friend from another land who is also seeking Bennu's help and that you know where to find her. Ten-ree will believe me because it is the truth, and if he believes me the others will."

Miranda did not argue with him. It was obvious that Iron Dog loved Ten-ree and wanted to believe in his perfect trust. But Miranda did not know the man, and moreover, now an outlaw herself, she was less and less inclined to trust anybody. Still, there was nothing to do but hope that he was right and that the outlaws would not choose to push her off the nearest cliff.

Iron Dog waited while Rattus and Naja clambered up Miranda to their places. "They won't see you?" he asked Bastable.

"You didn't—until I chose it," he replied.

"All right, then," said Iron Dog. "This way."

They crossed over the stream into the stand of trees, following the trilling of Ten-ree's flute. The sound, echoing off the cliffs and boulders, was deceptive, and they found the camp was farther away than they expected it to be. But at last, scrambling over a rocky knob, bathed in the late afternoon sun, they saw it in a bowllike depression below—one tent, several thick bedrolls, and a blackened circle of stones, around which sat a half-dozen adults and two children. Most were talking or eating. One was laying sticks in the stone circle. Another, a young woman, paced restlessly back and forth. The two children were playing a clapping game with great dexterity and speed. When one missed, the other rapped him on the head with her knuckles.

"None of that!" a man, sitting cross-legged, warned. In his hand was a flute.

Ten-ree, Miranda realized, taking in the very ordinary-looking profile, the average build. Then she moved slightly, cracking a twig. The flutist sprang to his feet, turning full face in her direction. Miranda flinched. His other profile was far from ordinary. It looked—the word came to her—*melted*.

"Who's there?" Ten-ree cried, hand on his knife. The other outlaws leaped up, drawing their weapons as well.

"The most humble reed can make the most beautiful music," Iron Dog called out.

A smile spread across Ten-ree's ravaged face. "The most humble man can conquer the world," he shouted back.

With a laugh, Iron Dog jumped down and strode over to his friend. Grasping Ten-ree about the waist, he lifted him high into the air. Ten-ree laughed too, hugging the boy and pounding his shoulders. The outlaws, grinning, gathered around, making comments such as, "You made it!", "Good to see you", and "Hope you brought some of those tasty pokuo eggs."

Iron Dog set down Ten-ree and glanced around. "Where are Chulo and Sparky?"

"They are still out searching. We have all been looking, but we have not yet found the benaves. Tomorrow we shall have to break this camp and try higher ground."

"Hey-ya! Gei-kwa?" one of the children called out, pointing up at the rocky knob from which Iron Dog had jumped. Everyone turned to look, immediately readying their weapons.

"That is my friend Miranda. She can help us find Bennu. Come down here, Miranda."

"Be careful, Miranda," warned Bastable, leaping forward.

Carefully, Miranda edged her way down and over to Iron Dog. At her side, Bastable growled softly.

"Your friend?" said a woman.

"Where did you meet this *friend?*" demanded a man.

"In the woods. Hiding from the Long Arms," Iron Dog improvised.

"She is not one of us." "How can you trust her?" "How dare you bring her to this camp?" other voices menaced.

Ten-ree's voice sliced through theirs. "If you know where Bennu is, tell us at once."

Miranda looked from one burning face to another and then up at Iron Dog. He laid a big hand on her shoulder. *But Naja told you*, she thought, *not me.* Iron Dog, reading her mind, gave her a warning look. "Go ahead, Miranda. Tell them," he said. She realized then why he was doing this. He was making her valuable to the outlaws.

"Don't tell them, Miranda," said Bastable. "I don't trust these people. We don't need their help. Let's go. We can come back for Iron Dog when we have found Bennu."

"Well, uh . . ." Miranda stammered in confusion. "Well . . ." Suddenly she heard Naja's voice in her head. "Ask to speak to Po-zhou," she said. Swallowing, Miranda drew herself up and said as authoritatively as she could, "I will tell no one but Po-zhou."

Iron Dog's fingers tightened on Miranda's shoulder and he looked at her in surprise.

Ten-ree turned to him. "You told her of Po-zhou," he said, almost accusingly.

Before Iron Dog had time to reply, a gravelly male voice asked, "Who speaks my name?" Everyone turned toward its source. The man was standing by the tent. He had been standing there, unnoticed, for some time. He was as tall as Iron Dog, but whereas the boy was broad and muscular, the man was whip-thin and wiry. His trim form marked him as a man in his thirties. But his weather-beaten face and steel-gray hair put him at sixty or more. Miranda guessed he was probably something in between.

Iron Dog led her to where Po-zhou stood. The older man squinted at him, nodding his head appraisingly. "You have made it after all," he said.

"Yes," the boy replied.

"And you brought a yin-jee."

There was a ripple of laughter behind them. Iron Dog reddened. "She's a friend, not a yin-jee."

"Oh, of course," Po-zhou apologized mockingly. "I beg your pardon. A strapping young man like you saves his ardor for revolution, not romance." The laughter increased, and this time Miranda blushed too. The man turned to her. "Who are you, girl, and where are you from?" he asked. "For it is certain you are not from around here."

"I am Miranda from Minnesota," she said, startled by the way the words popped out of her mouth.

"Hmmm. Never heard of it. Must be quite a ways from here."

"Quite a ways," she agreed, suddenly liking the man.

"Well, Miranda from Minnesota, come inside my tent and tell me what you know about the benaves," said Po-zhou. He held open the flap.

Miranda, Iron Dog, and Bastable followed him inside, and there she told him what Naja had said.

When she was done, Po-zhou stroked his chin. "The Moon Caves and the Cleft of Sirtis," he repeated.

"Yes, does it mean anything to you?"

He smiled faintly. "Yes, it means something. It is from an old legend. The story goes that on top of Silver Mountain at the hour of Wohar on the night of the Nesting Moon, three caves become visible. At the back of the middle cave is a small hole. In some tales, it is called the Breach of Tartian. In others, the Cleft of Sirtis. It is said that once every fifty-five years, when the moon is at its height, a comet casts a beam of light through the cleft. Whoever sees where the rays fall will find his or her heart's desire."

Iron Dog stirred excitedly. "Tonight is the Nesting Moon."

"And the comet, when is it due to appear?" asked Miranda.

Po-zhou cocked his head, bright eyes gleaming. "I will give you one guess," he said.

CHAPTER 19

The moon rose behind the great pinnacle of Silver Mountain, turning it glacial white. Though there was no time to lose, the small troop of rebels stood gazing up at it, allowing themselves a few moments' pause before the dizzying climb ahead.

Miranda hung back at the fringes of the group, watching Iron Dog, who was talking to Ten-ree. She knew her appearance had caused friction between the friends, a rift that even Po-zhou's support of her had not yet sealed. Iron Dog was trying to repair it now, and Miranda hoped for his sake he would succeed. Not only did she care about the boy, but she felt sympathy too for the older man.

A few hours earlier, as they sat waiting for the return of Chulo and Sparky, the two absent scouts, she had asked Iron Dog what had happened to his friend's face.

"Yes, he looks as though he were run over by a plow," added Bastable.

Miranda winced. Iron Dog let out a hard laugh, both at Bastable's bluntness and at the story he was about to tell. "A good guess," he said with the bitterness Miranda had heard before. "Except that it was a cart, not a plow, carrying ah-sha to the factory. His uncle was driving it too quickly, hurrying to get his pay. They rounded a corner. Ten-ree was thrown out. His uncle ran right over him. He did not even stop to help. Ten-ree lay there unconscious all day. How he got home he never knew. Weeks he spent in his bed, hovering between sleep and awakening. And when he did wake at last, he was a different man inside and out."

"That's terrible," Miranda said, shuddering. "No wonder he became an outlaw."

"Yes," Iron Dog replied, and fell silent.

"What about Po-zhou?" asked Rattus, his head peeking out of Miranda's pocket. "What's his story? How did he join your band?"

Iron Dog smiled slightly. The idea of a talking guapa was still absurd to him. But then he answered matter-of-factly, "Po-zhou did not join us—we joined him. He was not a farmer like the rest of us. He was—he is—a scholar and an historian, one of the few remaining. Many were killed in the Ah-sha Wars. But Po-zhou managed to flee. He is also a 'spirit-speaker.' It is said he conversed with Bennu the day she left the woods, and though she would not tell him where she was going, she promised he would see her again before he died. That hope has kept him alive for many years."

"How old is he?" asked Miranda.

"One hundred and two."

"No! That's impossible! He looks..." A sudden thought made her break off. "Is one hundred and two old here?"

"Very old. Is it old where you come from?"

"Very very old. I've never met anyone that ancient."

"Yesterday I reached five thousand six hundred and eighty-seven years," Naja said without a trace of bravado.

"Well, happy birthday!" said Rattus, making everyone laugh except the snake herself.

It was only Iron Dog and Ten-ree who were laughing now, softly. But the sound eased Miranda's heart. *Now if only something could ease me up that mountain*, she thought, as a muscle in her calf bunched and spasmed. She kneaded it with fingers too weary to do much good.

"Do you hurt much?" asked Naja.

"Enough."

"I am sorry I cannot take away the pain, but I am not a healer. Nor can I ease your burden by climbing the mountain on my own. It is too cold for me to move very far or very fast."

"I can climb on *my* own," said Rattus. "I'll stick to the shadows where no one can see me."

"Thanks, Rattus, but that won't be necessary. I can manage." Miranda stood up to follow the outlaws who had stopped their moon-gazing and started up the peak. Her leg throbbed when she put her weight on it, but she gritted her teeth and began the climb.

There were few trees now, and those were stunted, twisted things that clung precariously to the mountainside. The soil gave way to bare rock, worn so smooth in places, they had to crawl up it on their hands and knees. Po-zhou and the children, and of course Bastable, who was way ahead of the others, had the easiest time. Miranda had the hardest. She was dragging herself up over a jutting ledge when her toes slipped. She managed to hold on with her hands. Below was a fifteen-foot drop.

If she fell she would, at the very least, break an arm, a leg, or both. For a moment she dangled there, too frightened to scream. Then she felt strong hands grip her wrists and pull her slowly to safety. When her feet touched the ground, she found she was looking at Iron Dog's face.

"Are you all right?" he asked.

"Fine," she said. She took one step forward. Her legs buckled and she crumpled to her knees.

Rattus jumped from her pocket. "What happened?" he asked a bit shakily.

"I got tired," Miranda said.

"I think I really ought to walk now instead of hitch," said the rat, peering over the ledge.

"Okay," Miranda said woozily. "Go on then. I'll be up in a minute."

"We don't have a minute," said Iron Dog, helping her to her feet. "I will carry you."

"What? No, you can't . . ." she said. But she was too weak to argue. Iron Dog ditched his now-empty pack, fastened the basket to her back, and lifted her to his own. "Hold on," he instructed. "And don't let go."

He should have added, "Don't look down either." As the path wound up the mountain, it narrowed perilously close to the edge, revealing spectacular views of the valley and sheer drops not of fifteen but thousands of feet. To fall now would mean certain death. Miranda made the mistake of looking straight down. "Oh, my God," she moaned and clutched at Iron Dog, nearly pulling him off balance.

Only quick thinking and the refusal to panic saved them as Iron Dog managed to pitch forward and grab hold of one of the scraggly trees. Its rough bark covered his hands with sticky sap that would not come off entirely no matter how hard he rubbed.

After that, Miranda closed her eyes, buried her face against his neck, and did not move at all until they reached the summit.

Her first thought when she slid from his back and gazed around was, *Why does the top of this mountain look thin and pointed from the ground when it's actually broad and flat?* But she didn't think it was a question worth asking. Instead she said nothing.

In fact, no one spoke. The outlaws congratulated one another on reaching their destination by clasping shoulders or pressing palms. Iron Dog squeezed Miranda's hand. Rattus acknowledged them both by brushing against their legs before he hid behind a stone. Even Bastable was silent.

Then Po-zhou said, "It is the hour of Wohar." His voice, though quiet, was to the outlaws as loud as a trumpet blast. Tensely they stared at the moon, now at its apogee.

"Why are they looking at the moon?" jibed Bastable from behind Miranda. "Caves are not found in the sky."

Miranda turned, laying her finger on her lips to shush him. It was then she noticed the rocks. There were three of them, many times the height of Iron Dog. *Were they there before?* She wasn't sure. *Can they be the Moon Caves? No, that doesn't make sense.* These looked like solid boulders, not caves. And certainly not magical ones. If they were magical, Miranda imagined, their surfaces would sparkle in the moonlight and they would beckon you inside with a pearly luminescence.

Suddenly she gasped. The very image she had in her head was forming before her eyes. Now the glittering boulders were splitting open and rays of milky light were pouring from their depths.

"See," said Bastable. "I told you they wouldn't be in the sky."

"Look!" Miranda exclaimed. "Look! The Moon Caves."

Everyone turned at her cry. "There they are!" "The Moon Caves, there they are!" the outlaws chorused.

Ten-ree rushed forward, but Po-zhou pulled him back. "Let Iron Dog and his friend go first."

In the midst of her excitement and eagerness, Miranda frowned. She wished Po-zhou had not extended this courtesy. She could feel Ten-ree's own eagerness turn to impatience. She didn't want to provoke more trouble between him and Iron Dog than she'd already caused. But Iron Dog looked radiant as he came beside her. Slowly they walked to the entrance. Bastable was there before them, and Rattus too, slipping inside unnoticed.

The light grew no brighter as they entered. Instead it grew thicker and more opaque.

"I can't see anything," Miranda said.

"Nor can I," said Iron Dog.

Both expected Bastable to mock them, sneering at the limitations of human sight. But to their surprise, he murmured rather meekly, "I am blind here too. Are you, Rattus?"

"Yes," agreed the rodent, who'd slipped in beside them.

Then Naja spoke. "To see in the Moon Caves, you must close your eyes."

"What?" said Bastable. "That makes no sense at all."

"Do not argue," Naja reprimanded him. "Just do it."

He and the others obeyed. "It works!" Miranda exclaimed. "I can see all the way to the end of the cave. There is a small circle there and the moon is shining through."

"I see it as well," said Iron Dog, and Bastable and Rattus assented.

As they began to move toward it, they heard behind them the footsteps and voices of the outlaws. "Can't see. Can't see," they whimpered or complained. One of the children burst into tears.

"Close your eyes," Iron Dog called to them.

"Have you gone mad, my friend," Ten-ree called back.

"Do as he says," Po-zhou insisted.

Soon they all cried out in delight and amazement just as Miranda and her companions had.

Steadily they walked until they came to the end of the cave and the Cleft of Sirtis. "Think about your heart's desire," said both Naja and Po-zhou, one aloud, the other in Miranda's head. "Think well, and now, look!" Eighteen pairs of eyes opened in time to see a dazzling bolt of light shoot through the cleft and burst upon the dome of the cave, showering sparks like coins of gold. And in the shimmering haze remaining they all saw three great winged figures, larger than any eagle, brighter than any macaw, perched motionless on three wooden pedestals rising from the floor.

"The benaves!" "The benaves!" Sighs, hushed whispers, and the sound of soft, awed weeping filled the cave.

Po-zhou addressed the largest and most colorful of the creatures. "Bennu the Immortal, we have come to ask for your help. We ask you to call upon Chi-wa and Chi-na and all the other spirits to touch the people's hearts, to cleanse and restore our land and free us from the tyranny of ah-sha."

Naja slid from Miranda's waist to the ground and rose up before the benave. A startled murmur filled the cave when the outlaws saw her, but no one fled or moved to strike the snake.

"Bennu the Healer," Naja said. "We, the Correct Combination, ask that you join us and free our worlds from the tyranny of the Charmer."

All waited for the benave's reply. But she made none. Nor did she stir or open her eyes.

"Try again," said Ten-ree to Po-zhou.

"Try again," said Miranda to Naja.

"Empress, we beseech you. Awaken and heed our plea."

"Empress, we command you. Arise and join our cause."

Bennu remained still and silent in her dreamless sleep.

"What do we do now?" whispered Rattus.

"Will nothing awaken her?" asked Iron Dog.

Then a voice, low and insinuating, echoed through the cave. "Perhaps this will," it said.

The outlaws looked beyond the benaves to the man standing at the entrance. Most of his face and form were swathed in shadow. But what they could see, clear across the cave, were his long, flashing sword and his emerald green eyes.

CHAPTER
20

"It is Dee Lu Shen," Iron Dog breathed.

"It is the *Charmer*," Miranda warned. "Don't look at him. Don't look at his eyes." She reached up to shield him.

But he thrust her behind him, blocking her own view with his large frame. Neither of them saw Bastable slip through the wall of the cave and out of sight.

"Fools," said the prime minister as he advanced toward the rear of the cave. "Poor, deluded fools. Do you not see at last that the benaves will never help you. Have you not called upon them time and time again, to no avail. Here you stand, in grave danger, face-to-face, and still they will not come to your aid."

There was a faint, uneasy ripple among the outlaws. Dee Lu Shen saw it and went on. "The rest of the world is so much happier, believing these creatures to be dead. It would be a service to you to turn their belief into your reality." He took a few more steps forward, brandishing his sword.

The outlaws drew their own paltry weapons. Miranda could hear the scrape of steel against leather. "Naja, what do we do now?" she murmured.

"Take off the basket," the cobra replied, too quietly for Dee Lu Shen to hear.

"Are we going to leave without Bennu? *Can* we leave? Where can we go?"

"Take off the basket," the serpent repeated.

As Miranda hurriedly began to work at the knots, she heard Po-zhou's calm voice say, "You cannot kill the benaves. They are immortal."

Dee Lu Shen laughed. "Ah, Po-zhou. I might have known you'd be here. Well, old man, your belief that the benaves would help has proven untrue. Are you so sure this myth of immortality is not just one more lie?"

"I am sure. *We* are sure." Po-zhou glanced around, and his serenity gave the others strength.

"Yes," they said in unison. "We are sure."

Miranda's voice was not among theirs. She was concentrating on the knots. One had come undone easily enough, but the other was too tight. "Come on," she muttered. "Come on."

Suddenly near her ear, Rattus whispered. "Let me try."

She turned her head. He was perched on a stone jutting from the cave wall. Without hesitating, she backed up so he could gnaw the cord.

"Ah well, Po-zhou. Perhaps in this one thing you are right," Dee Lu Shen said. "However, you and your companions are far from immortal—a fact I shall now prove, starting with these children."

Ten-ree leaped out of the tight semicircle of outlaws. "There is only one of you—and many of us." He thrust out his knife twice, belly-level, in the air.

Dee Lu Shen stopped and smiled. Then he snapped his fingers. Instantly, the mouth of the cave was swollen with Long Arms, far outnumbering the outlaws. What path they'd taken to reach the mountaintop unseen no one knew. It was too late to matter anyway. The Long Arms began to move forward.

"Hurry," warned Naja.

"I'm hurrying as fast as I can," Rattus said through his busy teeth.

The prime minister snapped his fingers again and the soldiers halted. Then he lowered and leaned on his sword. "I am a merciful man," he said in his silky voice. "One who has never cared much for bloodshed—especially when it can so easily be avoided. You people are as annoying as tzumi flies—but just as harmless. Therefore, I can and will spare you—on one condition."

There was a long pause. Ten-ree glanced at Po-zhou. But the old man was looking at Bennu and he did not speak.

"What is the condition?" Ten-ree asked, still clutching his outthrust knife.

Once again, Dee Lu Shen smiled. "In exchange for your freedom, you will give me the girl called Miranda."

Into the uneasy silence two voices cried out. "No!" shouted Iron Dog. "Got it!" squeaked Rattus as the cord snapped in two and the basket slid almost noiselessly to the ground.

Around them, bodies shifted tensely, some involuntarily glancing their way. Rattus was in clear sight, but no one noticed him. They were all looking at Miranda. Ten-ree's expression was especially intent.

It took her a few seconds to realize what was happening, and then she felt herself go cold.

"No!" repeated Iron Dog. "You'll have to kill me first."

"That can be arranged, Iron Dog," said the Charmer, lunging forward with lightning speed.

But his sword never found its mark, for at that moment, Bastable fell through the ceiling of the cave and onto his back. The fenine tore at him with teeth and claws. It took no time at all for the Charmer to fling him halfway across the cave—but it was enough to allow Iron Dog to charge with his dagger and stab Dee Lu Shen through the heart.

Miranda gasped. *He's killed him. He's killed the Charmer,* she thought in amazement as the creature slumped to the ground. *We're free.* But her relief was short-lived, for with a bellow that shook the cave walls, the outlaws and Long Arms rushed at each other, and the battle began. The outlaws were armed only with knives and clubs, but they fought bravely and well. Ten-ree alone killed three Long Arms in quick succession. Bastable, who'd recovered quickly, gained possession of a sword, which he wielded quite well indeed. Rattus darted in and out of the fray, biting feet, ankles, calves, or whatever was nearest his sharp teeth.

"Naja!" Miranda cried, the two children cowering behind her. "Stop this! Can't you stop this? Now that the Charmer is dead."

The snake slid down her leg to the ground. "I alone can stop nothing, and the Charmer is not dead."

"What do you mean? I saw Iron Dog stab him through the heart."

"The Charmer has no heart," answered the snake, and she disappeared into the melee.

As Miranda stared in horror, the tide began to turn in favor of the Long Arms. Chulo collapsed, pierced in the belly by a soldier's sword. A young woman went down in a heap, skull split by her own club in the enemy's hand. Ten-ree's right shoulder streamed blood, though still he fought. Bastable was bleeding from a wound on his left hind leg.

Miranda glanced wildly around for Iron Dog and Rattus. She saw the boy, his chest dripping sweat, but not the rat. Iron Dog was fighting side by side with Po-zhou. The old man smashed a Long Arm across the neck with his club, and the man fell down. Miranda saw Po-zhou's look of astonishment at his show of strength. Then he jerked, and the look on his face changed to a new kind of astonishment. He reached around to touch his back and crumpled to the ground. Over him another Long Arm, sword point stained red, was laughing. But he did not laugh long. With a yell, he clutched at his leg. "Guapa!" he snarled. "Stinking little guapa!"

Iron Dog heard him, and spun around to hurl his dagger. But it stuck to some of the tree resin on his palm, delaying the throw. It gave the Long Arm time to thrust down his sword. Through the loud screams and cries Miranda heard a small, shrill squeal. She saw Rattus stumble out between the soldier's feet and fall.

"No!" she yelled. "Rattus, no!" Forgetting her own fear, she bolted to the rat and picked him up. He lay unmoving in her hands. "No," she sobbed. "You can't be dead, Rattus. You can't be."

"Oh, but he is," a soft voice said.

Miranda looked up. The Charmer was standing before

her. The sounds of the battle still raged behind him, but they seemed farther away.

"And I, as your friend the snake so acutely observed, am not."

Miranda knew she should be frightened, but all she could feel was anger and grief.

"I could have you join him, but I think, instead, it would give me more pleasure to allow you to live—here, where the sweet ah-sha will soon take away any pain or memory you have. Come, I know a quick path down this mountain." He reached for her arm.

But his hand froze as the sound of immense, long-silenced wings filled the cave. From her pedestal, Bennu, awake at last, was rising. She swooped at the Charmer and raked his cheeks with her claws.

He staggered back, covering his face. Again and again the benave struck at him.

"Look!" Miranda heard Ten-ree shout. "The benaves! The benaves are awake!"

Bennu's companions now flew into the air to attack the Long Arms. There were only two of them, but there might as well have been two hundred. They beat back the soldiers with wings, beaks, and talons. Shrieking, the Long Arms fled the cave.

Then the benaves turned to help Bennu. But the empress needed no help, for the Charmer had vanished.

The two benaves landed on their pedestals and gazed out at the remaining outlaws. Bennu landed on the ground near Po-zhou. The old man was still alive, but barely. His breathing was labored. His eyes were clouded with pain. Yet he managed to turn his head to the creature by his side and give a faint smile. "Thank you for keeping your promise," he said. Then he shut his eyes and did not open them again.

Bennu threw back her head and trumpeted one long, solemn note. The ceiling of the cave quivered and melted away. The benave flew to Miranda. With her talons she plucked Rattus from the girl's palms. Again she lifted her head and sang her note. Then she soared straight up and out of the cave into the night sky.

Miranda clenched her empty hands and wept. But the other two benaves left her little time to grieve. With sudden fierceness, they came at her, herding her backward. Iron Dog too they pushed, and Bastable. Soon the three found themselves near the basket.

The lid was off and Naja was sitting inside, looking oddly dazed.

"Naja, Rattus is . . ." Miranda said, but couldn't finish.

"Yesss," the snake slurred.

"And Bennu is gone. We . . . where can we go now? What can we do?"

"Not sssure. We just go."

"Iron Dog, what's happening? Where are the benaves taking you?" Ten-ree called out.

Iron Dog brushed away his tears. It was true, he knew now. Everything Miranda had told him about the Charmer was true. That meant that the Correct Combination was also fact. Except now the Correct Combination was destroyed, wasn't it? He turned to Miranda. She shook her head sadly, unable to answer his unspoken question. Then the boy looked at Ten-ree. "I will be all right, my friend. I pray we see one another again in happier times." Then he held out his hand.

Miranda took it. With her other, she reached for Bastable's paw.

Before they moved, Iron Dog said to the fenine, "I shall not forget that you saved my life."

Bastable nodded stiffly. "I shall not let you," he said.

Then together the three stepped into the basket.

CHAPTER
21

If Miranda had not been retching over the curb, she might have noticed that Iron Dog was about to be hit by a police car.

Bastable noticed and shouted to the boy to come back. Miranda's head shot up in time to see the car swerve around him and a red-faced cop shout out the window, "Hey, watch where you're going!"

"Oh, God!" she yelled, running out to pull Iron Dog out of the street. Things were going from bad to worse. First there was the ghastly basket ride, the effects of which she was still feeling. Once Miranda had been on a boat during a thunderstorm, and that had felt like a rocking chair compared to this. Worse was the fact that since it was Naja who steered the basket smoothly, the rockiness of this flight meant that something was wrong with the snake. What it was, Naja couldn't say. In fact she wasn't talking at all, just humming faintly and discordantly as she lay coiled in the basket. Miranda was not sure the cobra had even led them to the right place this time. How could Los Angeles in the year 2033—if the newspaper she'd seen was correct—be the right place?

Miranda managed to get Iron Dog back to the sidewalk where Bastable stood guarding the basket and Naja.

But the cop, flinging open the car door, followed.

"Just what the hell do you think you're doing?" the

corpulent man with slicked-down dark hair asked Iron Dog.

The boy stared blankly at him. The basket ride had not upset his stomach, but this city with its noise and motion was making his head spin.

"I said, What are you doing? *¿Que hace usted? ¿Comprende?*"

"He doesn't speak English or Spanish," Miranda explained reluctantly. "He's from a different country."

"He looks more like he's from a different planet." The policeman gave him the once-over.

"He's . . . he's a foreign exchange student," Miranda lied. "It's . . . it's his first day here."

"He's staying with you?"

"Yes."

The cop looked at her keenly. "And where do you live?"

Miranda tried to recall anything she'd read or seen about Los Angeles. What was it known for? Hollywood, Movie Capital of the World. But did anyone actually live in Hollywood? She wasn't sure. *Think, Miranda, what else makes Los Angeles famous? Disneyland. Great, tell him you live with Mickey Mouse, why don't you?*

The cop was getting impatient. "Uh . . . Beverly Hills," Miranda blurted out at last to him.

He eyeballed her slowly, clucking his tongue. She couldn't help but glance at herself as well. Her sweater —her dad's sweater—was filthy; her equally grubby pants were torn at both knees; her left sneaker had a hole in the toe. As for her face, hands, and hair, she knew they probably looked pretty awful as well.

"Beverly Hills, huh?" he said. "I live in Bel Air myself." He laughed sarcastically.

Miranda didn't get the joke, but she wisely said nothing.

Then the cop put his hands on her back and Iron Dog's. "Okay, get in the car, both of you. We're going down to the station to have a look at the Missing Persons file."

"No!" Miranda protested, too loudly. She didn't want to go down to the police station. She wasn't sure the cops would let her and Iron Dog go. "No," she said more calmly. "We are not Missing Persons. My name is Patsy Peabody. I live in Beverly Hills. Iron . . . I mean, Chao-ji is visiting here, and I don't think you're giving him a good impression of Americans at all."

"That's enough," the cop said with more boredom than anger. "Get in the . . ."

But his words were cut off by his partner, who stuck his head out the window and shouted, "A.P.B. Bank robbery. Mayer and Goldwyn."

Without another word to Miranda or Iron Dog, the cop ran into the car and it took off.

Miranda sighed, but her relief was fleeting. Iron Dog was looking at her with an expression that said, "This is your world. Teach me the rules."

I don't know the rules, she wanted to tell him. *I'm just a kid. I don't know how to survive in a city I've never been to, in a future I haven't even seen.* But she didn't say that because she felt it was her responsibility to take care of him here, just as he'd taken care of her in his world.

Okay, Miranda, think, she told herself. *Look around and*

think. What's different? What's the same? Let's see. The build-ings look the same and so do the trees. People's clothes look a little different, and those street lights are wild. So are the cars. That cop car was weird, all sleek and noiseless. But the cops were the same old cops, still fighting crime. What did they rush off to? A bank robbery. So people still hold up banks. Why? Because they still want money. "Money," she said aloud. "We need money. We won't be able to survive here without money."

She pulled out of her pocket a couple of bills, several coins, and a wisp of fur. Her lip quivered at the latter. *Rattus,* she grieved. Her eyes began to fill. *No,* she stopped herself from crying. *No time for that now.* She wiped her eyes, replaced the fur in her pocket, and counted the money. It came to two dollars and eighteen cents.

"Is that worth a lot?" asked Iron Dog, studying a dime.

"It wasn't in 1990 and it's probably worth even less now," Miranda replied.

"I do not understand this system of currency," said Bastable. "In Appledura we barter goods and services. For example, if you need a dish and I need a pillow, we trade."

"Bastable, even if that were to work here, we don't have anything *to trade.* We won't even be able to get jobs here in exchange for food. Even if I weren't too young, look at me. Who's going to hire me the way I look? I'm a mess."

"So, how will we get this money?" asked Iron Dog.

"Panhandle," Miranda answered.

"What does that mean?"

"Beg."

Bastable let out a short, horrified yowl. "*Beg*. You are expecting us to beg?"

"I'm not expecting you to do anything but annoy . . . I mean, keep us company and watch Naja and the basket. Iron Dog and I will beg . . . *panhandle*—until we can at least pay for a meal. Then we'll worry about shelter," Miranda told him resolutely. But inside she thought, *I'm worried right now.*

The panhandling did not go well. At first Miranda thought maybe they were in the wrong place—too many private houses, not enough pedestrians. So they walked and walked until they came to an area with more sidewalk traffic. She noticed there were other panhandlers around, so she took that as a good sign. It wasn't. The people strolling by had had their fill of panhandlers, and most either ignored them or were mildly rude. Others, who might have been more generous, did not know what to make of Iron Dog, who could not speak but only dumbly hold out his hand. After two hours, they had taken in only one dollar and six cents in change that looked as if it was made of plastic, and it was starting to get dark.

Iron Dog gave Miranda a searching look. "We haven't been successful, have we?" he asked.

"No."

"Perhaps we'll do better tomorrow. I'm not very hungry now anyway. You may use my share for yourself."

Miranda didn't have the heart to tell him there wasn't enough there to buy a rat a meal. She felt her eyes watering again. *I'm so useless*, she thought. *I didn't do anything to save Rattus. I don't know what to do for Naja. I can't even help Iron Dog or Bastable get some food.* "I'm not hungry either," she said.

"Well then, maybe we should find shelter."

"Shelter," Miranda repeated, trying to keep the anxiety out of her voice.

"Yes. It is warm here. We do not have to go indoors. We could lie under a tree. I saw a small forest nearby."

"You did?"

"He means that park we passed," Bastable said.

"Oh." Miranda didn't know what to say. She knew homeless people often slept in parks or on beaches. Yes, that was another thing she'd heard about Los Angeles. It had great beaches. If she could find one, they might be able to sleep there. At least the sand would be soft. "Excuse me." She stopped a passerby. "Can you direct us to the beach?"

The teenaged girl looked at her as if she were screwy. "It's right down there," she said.

"Where?"

"Down that street, bluto."

Miranda had never heard the word *bluto*, but she figured it shared a similar definition with *dweeb* or *jerk*. Still, she politely said, "Thank you." When the girl had gone she scooped up the basket. From it, Naja's voice drifted out, "Movies beguile."

"What?" said Bastable. "What did she say?"

"Naja, are you okay?" asked Miranda.

"Movies beguile," the serpent repeated.

"Yes. But are you all right?" Miranda had no idea what she was talking about.

"All right. Must sleep," the cobra replied and fell silent.

Miranda's anxiety increased, but she did not let it show. "I have a better idea than the park," she told Iron Dog and Bastable. "Follow me." And she led them down the street.

A long pier lined with homey cafes and shops rolled out over the sand, a wooden carpet welcoming them to the Pacific Ocean. Bastable was not much impressed— the Plumbean Sea off the west coast of Appledura was much more formidable, he said. But Miranda, who had seen the ocean only in the movies, was, and as for Iron Dog, who had seen only ponds and streams, he was astounded.

"Does it end?" he asked.

"Of course," Miranda told him.

"Where?"

"Very far from here."

"How far?"

"I'm not sure. Thousands of miles, at least."

"How deep is it?"

"Very deep."

"Over my head?"

Bastable snorted with condescension. But Miranda, remembering a book she'd once seen, patiently said, "The ocean is so deep that sunlight can't get to the lower depths. There are fish down there that glow in the dark."

Iron Dog's eyes widened. "I would like to see that," he said.

Miranda had the sudden desire to hug him, the way one would a young child. "I would too, someday," she admitted.

For a while they gazed in silence at the waves. Around them bits of conversation floated like flecks of foam:

"So, I said to him, 'My hair's as real as your teeth.' "

"The Moochy Club? The Moochy Club is out! They don't even have a centrifugal laser swarm."

"I do like you, Dennis. Just not as much as you like me."

"I'd kill for tickets to the Hypnodrome opening. *Kill* . . ."

"What do you want, Japanese or Mexican?"

Soon the voices, the conversation faded away as the stars grew brighter in the moonless sky. Miranda, Iron Dog, and Bastable, with Naja in tow, made their way beneath the pier. Some people were already sleeping there, wrapped in tatty blankets or cast-off beach towels that had seen better days.

They found an untenanted spot. Iron Dog laid down the heavy cloak he'd still been wearing. They stretched out upon it, spreading Miranda's cloak over them like a quilt, and let the shush of the surf lull them to sleep.

CHAPTER 22

Miranda knew the girl was watching her. She'd been watching for at least fifteen minutes. Trying to ignore her, Miranda walked up to a man in a T-shirt that read IT'S ALL IN YOUR MIND—OR IS IT? HYPNODROME. APRIL 1, 2033, and went into her pitch. It was a good pitch—short, bold, to the point. She'd been perfecting it over the past five days—with the unwitting help of several other seasoned panhandlers.

"Have a heart, sir. Help a poor girl return to the twentieth century," it went, accompanied by an outstretched hand in which rested a 1988 dime. It nearly always worked, sometimes better than she expected. This was one of those times.

"Look at that," the man in the T-shirt said. "Where'd you get that?"

"From my mother, the last time I saw her—forty-three years ago."

The man laughed. "Cute. Very cute. Well, how about I give you forty-three bucks for it?"

Miranda tried to act blasé. Forty-three dollars was a considerable chunk of money to her. But she wasn't sure it was enough. After all, the dime might be worth more —a possibility she'd considered but hadn't had time to explore. Secondly, it was the dime that was her lucky charm, her magnet, drawing in the cash. No, she decided.

It wasn't wise to part with it. "Sorry, the dime's not for sale," she said, waiting to see if the man upped his offer.

He didn't. "Okay." He reached into his pocket, pulled out three unos, as singles were now popularly called, and handed them to her. "Thanks anyway for the look," he said good-naturedly and walked away.

When he was out of sight, Miranda kissed the bills. She felt good today. Things were looking up. Last night Iron Dog had gotten a job washing dishes at a small restaurant. The previous dishwasher had just quit. The desperate owner, seeing the tall, strong boy with Miranda on the street, practically dragged him inside. The fact that the boy could not speak English or produce documents of any kind referring to his country of origin or his legal right to live or work in the United States did not faze the man. "As long as he gets those dishes good and clean and doesn't break more than a half dozen or so, I don't care if he's from Mars," he said. The salary was not high, but Iron Dog would get free dinner. Last night he'd given half of it to Miranda. The chef saw him do it and felt sorry enough to offer him any leftovers that were not to be otherwise recycled.

The promise of at least one regular meal was a great relief to Miranda since up till then all of their meals had been erratic at best, a combination of whatever their meager finances would allow them to afford and the things Bastable could steal. He'd become quite adept at pilfering—if not always at what to pilfer. He took some things simply because he liked the labels. Miranda learned this during their second evening on the beach when among the items in his cache she discovered a can of Cat's Paw shoe polish, featuring a sleek black feline on the lid. Though she questioned him carefully about it, she did not criticize him for taking the can. First of all, he'd also managed to swipe a remarkable number of comestibles and other useful items. Second, she knew that as he could only smuggle one or two things at a time from the store to the beach, he'd had to have been at it all day long. So she just thanked him lavishly and was rewarded with a rare fenine purr.

Well, he deserves a reward and so does Iron Dog and so do I, she thought, looking at the bills in her hand. She did not include Naja in her thoughts. It was too painful. The snake was no better, although no worse, than she'd been, and Miranda was afraid she'd be that way forever—like a distant cousin of hers who spent her days in her room talking to the ceiling. Shoving the bills into the pocket of her "new" shorts, purchased at Fuggy's Thrift Shop, she decided with what she'd made last night and this morning she had enough to treat her friends to a proper sit-down coffee shop breakfast. Iron Dog still did not know what French toast was. Bastable had not had a sausage in a very long time. Of course, he'd have to eat it off her plate when the waitress wasn't looking. Grinning, she set out to wake them and almost bumped right into the girl. "You still here? What do you want from me?" she said, rather gruffly because the girl had startled her.

"I don't want anything from you," the girl responded, looking straight at Miranda with large, smoky blue eyes that contrasted strikingly with her nutmeg-colored skin.

"I want to give you something." Her smile was friendly, but not overly familiar. I know where you're at, it seemed to say, but I won't bug you about it.

"If it's money, I'll take it," Miranda said baldly. She didn't have time for beating around the bush these days. She'd learned that it got you nowhere on the street.

"It's not exactly money. It's a token. A bus token," the girl said, holding it out along with a piece of paper. "And these are directions."

Unwillingly, Miranda found her curiosity was piqued. "To where?" she asked reluctantly.

"To the Sanctuary."

"The what?"

"The Sanctuary. It's a home for runaways."

"I'm not a runaway," Miranda said with a lot of defiance and more than a little fear. Since that run-in five days ago, she'd managed to avoid the cops. But they were constantly in her mind. Though she couldn't say why she was certain, she felt sure that if the cops took them in, any hope of returning to their own worlds would be lost.

"Sure. Okay. You're not a runaway," the girl said. "But all the same, if you need a place to sleep—even for one night—you can come here, any time of the day, no questions asked." She was still holding out the token and the directions.

Miranda stared at them for a long moment. Then, with a shrug, she took them. "Thanks," she mumbled without much grace.

"You're welcome," the girl said and started to walk away.

"Hey!" Miranda called after her. "You work there?"

The girl turned. "I live there," she said, with that same smile.

Miranda did not let her surprise show. Instead, she nodded. "Okay. Well, see you around maybe."

"See you around," replied the girl, and she moved on.

Miranda looked down at the directions. "The Sanctuary. 37188 Santa Casa Street," she read. Underneath was one more word—"Skye." Miranda picked up her head. She could just see the girl's long, dark, crinkly braid as she turned a corner. Skye. How old is she? Sixteen? Seventeen? Miranda shrugged again and began to crumple the piece of paper. But instead she changed her mind and put it in her pocket, right next to the lucky dime.

SCIENCE-FICTION FESTIVAL

TONIGHT: STAR WARS

read the marquee, which was festooned with brightly flashing lights. Shifting the basket in her arms, Miranda sighed. *Star Wars.* How many times had she seen that movie? And now, forty years into the future, kids her age could still see it. She wondered if they were going to see it, though. The show was starting in a few minutes and there wasn't much of a crowd; what people were entering the cinema weren't kids but grown-ups around her grandparents' age. With a start, Miranda realized they had probably been kids when the movie opened and had seen it then in a theater. *I bet they were so excited,* she thought, looking at a pleasant-faced, gray-haired couple. *I bet he imagined he was Han Solo and she wanted to be just like Princess Leia.* Miranda smiled with fondness for these people she didn't even know.

"You want to go in there?" asked Bastable, pulling her out of her reverie.

"Yes," Miranda replied. "But I can't."

"Why not?"

"No money." Breakfast, laundry, and the jeans and shirt she'd bought for Iron Dog had wiped them out. "And no time," she added. "Iron Dog gets off work soon. We've got to pick him up." Miranda gave one last wistful look at the cinema and sighed.

"Look at that. Science-Fiction Festival. That's so retroid," a young woman said to her date as they passed by.

"Really. That's old frommage. The Hypnodrome is the neuve," he replied. "I can't wait to go."

The Hypnodrome, Miranda puzzled, watching them walk on. *What the heck is the Hypnodrome.* She'd been hearing about it all week. "Hypnodrome," a voice repeated. It was Naja's, and it startled Miranda. The snake spoke little these days, and much of what she said was garbled. Suddenly Miranda felt hope rise in her. Maybe the snake was going to be all right after all. Maybe she knew why they were in Los Angeles and what they had to do to leave. "Do you know what it is, this Hypnodrome?" Miranda whispered through the lid.

"Movies beguile," was the cobra's reply.

"What does that mean, Naja? You've said it before. Please tell me, what does it mean?" Miranda begged.

But the serpent didn't answer. And Miranda's hope gave way to such a bleak sadness she had to shake herself to dispel it. Then she and Bastable went to meet Iron Dog.

He was just finishing up when they reached the restaurant. Juan Alexis, the chef, had given him enough leftovers for a nice little feast.

"Tell your boyfriend he's a good worker," he told Miranda.

"He's not my boyfriend, but I'll tell him anyway." She smiled.

"What you got in that basket? Laundry?"

"That's right," Miranda lied.

"You must do a lot of it. You were lugging that thing around last night too."

Miranda smiled again, but said nothing. Iron Dog took the basket from her, and in another minute they, and Bastable, were heading for home—which is how they were beginning to view their patch of sand under the pier. As yet no one had disturbed them there. Their neighbors didn't talk much, but they kept an eye on one another's property and would not tolerate stealing. Miranda found they could leave their "bedding" there and not worry about it disappearing. She did not, however, feel safe about the basket, which is why she took it with her whenever she left.

"Did you have a good evening?" Iron Dog asked as they trotted down the steps onto the beach.

"Not bad. And you?"

"Okay," he answered in English, making Miranda grin.

"Food smells good," she said.

"Yes."

They were under the pier now. Iron Dog had a little flashlight he'd found to light the way to their place. It was he who first noticed something was wrong. "Where is everybody?" he said. "It is not late, but they are usually here by now."

"You're right," Miranda responded. "Where are they?"

Suddenly, there was a movement near one of the posts. Iron Dog swung his flashlight around. A stooped figure sifted out from the shadows. It was one of what the other beach people called the "permanents," an elderly woman who'd been living there so long no one knew if she'd ever had another home.

"Roundup," she said in a surprisingly melodious voice.

"What?"

"Cops coming. Round up the beachers. They all split. You better go too."

"Oh, no," Miranda said. "Are you sure?"

"Honey, Annie doesn't lie."

"Well, then, why are you still here?"

"Annie got nowhere else to go."

"Neither do we," Miranda said.

But the old woman was already hobbling farther along the sand.

"What's the matter?" asked Iron Dog. "What has she told you?"

"That we can't stay here anymore."

"Must stay," Naja rasped suddenly and with agitation.

"What?" Miranda's voice rose, half in fear, half in frustration.

"Must stay. Reunion. Beach. Reunion. Beach. Must stay."

"Naja, what are you talking about?"

"Movies beguile."

"Oh, no," Miranda snapped. "Not that again."

In the distance, a siren began to blip.

"Oh, no," Miranda repeated, shoving her hands nervously into her pockets. Her fingers found her lucky dime, and next to it, a crumpled piece of paper. She took it out and looked at it under Iron Dog's flashlight. "No choice," she murmured.

"Must stay," muttered Naja.

Shut up, Miranda nearly shouted at her. But instead, she said, "Okay. I know a place we can go. We have to take a bus. But we'll be safe there." To herself she added, *I hope.*

CHAPTER
23

"Are you sure this is the place?" asked Bastable as they stood on the steps of the large modern house on the quiet residential street.

"It had better be," Miranda answered. They'd had to spend just about all their money for a bus token for Iron Dog, who had not yet gotten his pay. The trip had taken half an hour. So here they were at midnight in an unknown, unexplored neighborhood with no cash. If the Sanctuary didn't take them in, they would have to spend the night on the grass like oversized lawn ornaments, and Miranda didn't think the neighbors would take too kindly to that. Still, she hesitated before ringing the bell and looked at Iron Dog. What would they make of him here? Miranda was certain they would not be allowed to share a room. He did all right at the restaurant, but everybody was too busy to bother him much there. Here she suspected the kids had plenty of time to get under one another's skin.

Iron Dog caught her look. "What is it?" he asked.

"Some of the kids here might not be too nice to you," she said.

"None of the 'kids' in my land were nice to me—or anyone else," he said quietly.

She nodded and rang the bell.

The woman who answered was petite as a gymnast,

and, Miranda thought, probably just as strong. Her smooth brown face, darker than Skye's, with its high cheekbones and large eyes might have been called fragile if it didn't bear such a crisp, no-nonsense expression. She looked Miranda and Iron Dog up and down.

"This . . . this is the Sanctuary, isn't it?" Miranda said, finding herself annoyingly tongue-tied. She did not want to appear helpless before this woman.

"Yes, it is."

"Skye told me . . . us . . . we could come here any time. . . ."

Without answering, the woman reached into her pocket and pulled out a small rectangular object resembling a VCR remote control. She pressed a button and spoke into it. "Skye. Two NA's." Then, she opened the door wider to let in Miranda, Iron Dog, and, without knowing it, Bastable and Naja. "Skye will be down soon. She will show you to your rooms. If you're hungry, I'll take you to the kitchen. Mr. Bonami is gone for the evening, and Jeff, who's assisting him this week, has gone to bed. But we can scrounge up something."

"We've eaten," Miranda told her flatly.

The woman nodded and ushered them through the mirrored vestibule into a rather elegant and comfortable sitting room. Miranda sank into the sofa with a small sigh, holding the basket on her lap. She'd almost forgotten what it felt like to sit on furniture.

"What are your names?" the woman asked, sitting across from her.

"I'm Patsy and this is Chao-ji. He doesn't speak English or Spanish," she said with a tone that did not welcome further questions.

The woman gave Miranda a penetrating look as if she wanted to know whether or not the girl was as tough as she was making herself out to be. Hard as it was, Miranda stared right back until the woman smiled and said, "My name is Ms. Saunders. I run this place. We have few rules here, but we enforce them. NA's—new arrivals—are welcome in at any time. But no one is allowed to stay out past ten P.M. without informing me first. Breakfast is from seven to eight. Lunch from twelve to one. Dinner from six to seven. It's Easter vacation now, but in a few days, if you choose to stay, we'll talk about school. If you reside here longer than a week, you are thereafter assigned a weekly task and you get a weekly allowance for doing it. Skye's task this week is to help NA's. And here she is now."

Dressed in a long, flowing blue robe, Skye entered the room. Her thick curly hair, now unbraided, billowed out over her shoulders, and her blue eyes shone with genuine pleasure. She was very pretty, Miranda noticed. She looked sideways at Iron Dog, wondering if he noticed it too.

"I'm glad you decided to come," Skye said. She turned to Iron Dog, who was smiling a bit shyly. "And that you brought a friend."

Miranda muttered her agreement and gratitude.

"There's a spare bed in Ramon's room. Your friend can stay there. And you can stay with me. That is, if you don't mind a little snoring." She grinned.

Miranda nearly grinned back. There was something about this girl that made you want to smile, the way Rattus always did. Remembering the rat made Miranda tighten her mouth. *Be careful*, she told herself. *Don't let her get too close. You don't know who she is. You don't know whether you can trust her—or anybody here.* She dropped her eyes from Skye's and shrugged.

The older girl led them upstairs, telling them in a low voice about the house. It was a donation, she said, from a well-to-do producer who had himself been a runaway. "That's why every room has a Telewall," she explained.

"A what?" Miranda couldn't help asking.

"A Telewall. You don't mean to say you don't know what that is."

"Sure I do," Miranda declared. "I just didn't hear what you said."

Skye pointed out the bedrooms and then the two bathrooms. She also gave them pajamas and a nightshirt from what she called, with amusement, the "wardrobe," and towels from the linen closet. Iron Dog took his things and disappeared into one bathroom where he washed quickly in the sink.

"Here, I'll put this in our room while you wash up," Skye said to Miranda, reaching for the basket.

"No, that's all right," Miranda said, holding onto it with one hand and grabbing the towel and nightshirt with the other.

If Skye found this behavior eccentric, she didn't let on. "Okay," she said. "Well, see you later." She walked into her room. Bastable followed her.

In the bathroom, Miranda set down the basket on the toilet seat, then filled the tub and settled in with a sigh. She never took baths at home—just showers. Baths had always seemed like a waste of time. But now she thought she could probably spend the whole night in the tub. The water was so soothing, and besides, she hoped Skye would be asleep by the time she got out.

But Skye was very much awake. She was reading a book, but she put it down when Miranda came into the room. Bastable, however, was curled up on Miranda's bed, fast asleep.

Miranda set down the basket in a corner and got under the covers.

"Your boyfriend's cute," Skye said conversationally. "Unusual looking, but cute."

"He's not my . . . Yeah, he is cute."

"He seems nice too."

"Yeah."

"I had a nice boyfriend once. At least I thought he was. My mom didn't want me to see him because he was not only five years older than me, but he was also Protein-Active. I didn't care what she said. I was crazy about him and he said he was crazy about me. I should have known better with a Techhead. Anyway, then he told me he was going to move away, but that he'd wait for me till I was legal. Well, I didn't want to wait till I was legal, so I left home to find him. . . ." Skye paused.

Miranda waited silently for her to go on.

"And I did," she said at last. "We had two great months together. Then one day I came home from this housecleaning job I had, and there was this note: 'Went to join the Stellar. Sorry. I love you. Jesse.' A Techhead. Just like my mother. It was the only thing they had in common." She sighed.

Though Miranda didn't understand all of the details of the story ("Protein-Active"? "The Stellar"? "Tech-head"?), she'd followed the plot well enough. "He didn't come back?" she asked carefully.

"Nope," Skye answered. "And I didn't go home. Living with my mother had always been Slave City. I knew if I went back it would be even worse. So I became a beacher. Just like you. Until somebody told me about this place." She smiled her engaging smile again. This time it was full of expectation. She had just spilled her guts and was giving Miranda the opportunity to do the same. There was nothing pushy about her attitude, and that attracted Miranda, tempting her to do what Skye wished.

Well, it's like this, Miranda imagined herself saying. *I was minding my own business one day—me and my invisible friend, Bastable, who's right here on my bed—when Naja—the snake in this here basket—dragged us off to fight the Charmer. Then we met Rattus, who's dead, and Iron Dog—Chao-ji to you—and Bennu, who wouldn't come with us. Something's wrong with Naja, so maybe we shouldn't even be here in Los Angeles. But we are and we don't know what's going to happen to us. And . . ."* Miranda stifled a sound that was somewhere between a laugh and a sob. *No. No crying. You're tough, Miranda. You've got to stay tough.* But the warm bath, the soft bed, the friendly girl were cracking the wall she'd built around herself for the past five days, and the tears began to trickle down her cheeks.

Skye handed her a cotton handkerchief. "No tissues here," she said. "Ms. Saunders is a Woodsie."

Miranda wiped her eyes and blew her nose. "Thanks," she mumbled. She still hadn't told Skye anything, but the girl didn't seem to mind. *There's plenty of time*, her eyes said.

After Miranda stopped weeping, Skye asked, "Want to watch Telewall? Technically, it's lights out, but nobody's going to hassle us tonight, as long as we keep the volume low."

"Okay," Miranda agreed.

Skye sat up in bed and looked at the opposite blank wall. "Tele on," she enunciated and clapped her hands three times. A dot of light beamed onto the center of the wall and expanded quickly to fill the entire space with a moving picture of a car chase. Miranda was pleasantly startled. "Wow," she said under her breath.

"Ugh. Boring," said Skye. "Let's try channel ten." Again, she pronounced the words, but this time she didn't have to clap. One by one she flicked channels just by saying the number until she found a talk show. The host was interviewing a handsome young actor. "Stim Severance," Skye said with a contented sigh. "What a delecto." She settled back to watch.

Miranda watched too. The Telewall was amazing. It was like having these people right in the room. But when it became apparent that both the host and the actor were not folks she especially wanted in her room, her interest began to flag. She wondered if the next guest would be more interesting. But she wasn't.

So Miranda was nearly asleep when Skye's voice buzzed in her ears, "Hypnodrome, Hypnodrome, Hypnodrome. Boy, am I sick of Hypnodrome hype. I mean, talk about the ultimate Techhead trash. Telewall off." She began to clap her hands once, twice . . .

"Wait," said Miranda, suddenly awake. "I'd like to see this, if you don't mind."

Skye shrugged. "Okay."

As Miranda watched, the host finished showing footage of people lining up to buy Hypnodrome tickets for the "most exciting media event of the century," to be held the very next evening, and then said, "Now, a rare treat. Our third guest is none other than the creator of Hypnovision and the Hypnodrome, the distinguished filmmaker/inventor Bentley Gyle."

There was loud applause from the studio audience as the smartly dressed man with the trim moustache stepped out from behind the curtain and onto the stage. He smiled jauntily at the camera, which glared off his elegant black-rimmed eyeglasses, and sat opposite the host.

"Such a pleasure to have you here," he gushed.

"It's a pleasure to be here," the man replied.

"Now, *American Media* has called Hypnovision 'the first and only interface between real life and art.' What do you think of that?"

"I agree with it. Hypnovision purposely blurs the division between fact and fiction to create an entirely new —and, may I add, improved—reality."

"Ah, yes. 'Improved.' There's a word that has gotten you into some trouble with, er, *Vox Populi*, which says, 'The Hypnodrome could well prove to be the most dangerous invention since the atom bomb.' What comments can you offer about that?"

"Well, that quote is obviously the result of counter-visionary consciousness—exactly the sort Hypnovision hopes to change on a grand scale. By that I mean Hypnovision is not some arty intellectual experiment for the elite; it's High Entertainment for Everyone."

The audience cheered and applauded loudly. Skye clucked her tongue. "Something about that man bothers me," she said. "And it's not just that he's a Techhead."

"And now," the host announced when the cheering died down, "we have a big surprise." His voice quavered with excitement. "Exclusively on our show—an actual sneak preview of the Hypnodrome's first feature in Hypnovision, *Mindspin*."

The cheers and applause rose to a remarkable pitch, and then everyone went abruptly silent. A disclaimer rolled onto the screen which said, "As Hypnovision can be fully experienced only in the setting of the Hypnodrome, this segment is not to be taken as a true replication of the Hypnovision experience." The words disappeared and the screen went momentarily dark. Then suddenly it was filled with swirls of color. Red, blue, orange, purple. The camera pulled back to reveal that the rainbow was a group of brightly dressed children playing a circle game. As they spun around, laughing, Miranda found a warm feeling of well-being seeping through her. She began to laugh with the children. "Whee," she called lightly. "Whee!" Suddenly, she was no longer in the room, but there with them. A boy held one of her hands, a girl the other. "Faster," said the boy. "Run faster." Miranda hastened to obey. Her legs pumped, pumped till she thought she was flying. "Whee!" she shouted, so, so happy. At last they all collapsed on the ground, giggling, cuddling. "Love"—the word floated into Miranda's brain as she lay with her head on another child's tummy. "Peace. Love."

Then something changed, like a sudden chill wind rippling through an August night. Miranda and the children slowly sat up and glared at one another. "You pinched me." "You squashed me." "You bluto." "You creep." The epithets became nastier. Threats were made. "I hate you, scumwacker." "I'll smash you, leptarded merdemouth." "Bust your jaw." "Kick your conies." Miranda felt her lips pull back in a snarl. "Spratsucker!" she screamed as the word "Hate" burned hot and red in her brain. She hauled back her fist to punch the child she'd snuggled with just a moment before, when all at once the screen went black.

A moment later, Miranda, blinking, found herself sitting on the bed, slowly uncurling her fists. What had just happened? What was that? She glanced at Skye. The girl was looking back at her with a stunned expression. "Jeez," she said. "Jeez."

"Well, that was quite something," the host's voice interjected brightly.

Miranda and Skye both turned back to the screen. The man's eyes were somewhat glazed and his upper lip was beaded with sweat. The camera panned the audience, all somewhat dazed looking. They began to applaud tentatively.

Then the camera focused on Bentley Gyle. The man gazed at it and said with a twinkle, "It's all in your mind—or is it?" Smiling, he took off his glasses and winked, and this time the lens captured the color of his intensely green eyes.

"Oh, God. Oh, my God," said Miranda, gripping and twisting the quilt in her hands. From the set issued the approving roar of the audience. "It's him. It's . . ."

"Movies. B. Gyle," said Naja in Miranda's head. And this time Miranda knew exactly what she meant.

CHAPTER
24

"Skye?" Miranda, propped on one elbow, whispered. "Skye?"

In her bed across the room the girl stirred slightly, but did not awaken.

At last, Miranda thought. She'd been waiting for what seemed like hours for Skye to fall asleep. Turning to Bastable, she shook him lightly. He awoke immediately. "We have to go," she murmured in his ear.

"Why?" he asked.

"Tell you later."

"All right." He got up and waited by the door as Miranda slid out from under the covers and began to pull on her clothes.

A few hours before she'd had to do some fast talking to explain her reaction to Bentley Gyle, claiming it was the lingering effects of "that weird movie."

"It was weird, all right. Like taking halludrugs or something." Skye shuddered with what Miranda sensed was both alarm and fascination.

Miranda bit her lip in an effort not to blurt out the truth about Bentley Gyle's nasty new invention—that, unless she was very much mistaken, Hypnovision in its full-length, total Hypnodrome glory *was* a drug, one that would not wear off. Skye would never believe it anyway, she told herself, and just nodded with both sadness and relief that she'd escaped detection.

But no fast talking would help her now if Skye awoke and saw what she was doing. Fully dressed, Miranda was quickly and quietly rifling through the girl's purse, which was lying on the dresser. Pocketing the wad of bills she'd extracted, she picked up the basket and turned to Skye's bed. She'd never stolen a thing in her life and she hated doing it now—especially from someone who'd been so kind. But she could see no other choice. "I'm sorry," she whispered. Easing open the door, she and Bastable slipped out of the room.

The figures occupying the two beds in the room they entered both had blankets pulled over their heads. *Which one is Iron Dog*, Miranda wondered tensely. She chose the bed on the left and, holding her breath, plucked the cover delicately off the person lying there. The streetlight shone dimly on a long, thin, and unfamiliar face. Miranda dropped the blanket back over it and tiptoed to the other bed. Bastable was already there, his paw over Iron Dog's startled mouth.

"We have to go," the fenine told the boy, who was staring with a panic-stricken look.

But Iron Dog's fear disappeared rapidly and he nodded. Bastable removed his paw. Then the boy sprang out of bed soundlessly. Miranda turned her head while he stripped off the pajamas he was wearing and hurried into his clothes. A moment later, he, Bastable, and Miranda found themselves out in the dark hall.

The thick carpeting muffled their footsteps as they stole down the stairs and into the mirrored vestibule. *Funny*, Miranda realized. *I can see Bastable next to me, but I can't see him in that mirror. I wonder if he can see himself?* But she decided to save the question for another time. They had more urgent matters to attend to.

Iron Dog with his long strides reached the front door first, but the complicated locks eluded him. They nearly eluded Miranda as well until she realized all she had to do was press a button near the strike. *Click*, the locks slid open. Miranda seized the knob, willing the door not to creak.

It didn't, opening instead without a whisper. When it shut again behind them they heard a second click as the locks shot back in place. They all breathed deeply.

Then Bastable demanded, "All right. What happened? Something did happen, didn't it? Something involving the Charmer?"

"Something happened," Miranda agreed. "The Charmer's here. The Correct Combination is not complete, but we three have still got to do something, and I think I know what. I'll tell you on the way."

"Where are we going?" asked Iron Dog.

"To the Hypnodrome. I don't know where it is, but I'm sure someone will tell us where to find it."

"Yes, someone will tell you," said Skye, stepping out from behind the dense jade trees by the door.

Miranda let out a strangled cry. Iron Dog drew his knife and just as quickly sheathed it.

"Come on," said Skye, seizing Miranda's arm and pulling her away from the house.

Miranda resisted. "What are you doing? You're not going to call Ms. Saunders?"

"No. I'm going with you—to the Hypnodrome."

"You can't."

"Why not? I'm paying for all our fares, aren't I?" Skye looked pointedly at Miranda's pocket.

"I'm sorry. I'll return the money, I swear. But you can't go with us."

Above them a light flickered on in the house. "If we stand here arguing none of us will go anywhere," said Skye.

"The human's right," said Bastable. "Hurry."

Miranda looked at Iron Dog. He nodded, and then they all ran down the sidewalk and up the street.

"What is that Bentley Gyle person to you? I saw the way you acted when you saw him—and don't hand me that line about being hung over from Hypnovision. He isn't your father, is he?" Skye asked as they rode an empty Electrobus through the quiet streets.

"No," Miranda half laughed, half spat.

"I didn't think so. But he is someone you know. Someone who did something nasty to you. You called him a charmer—but not with affection."

"Yes," said Miranda.

"And you want to get back at him by messing up his big premiere, right?"

"That's right," Miranda agreed cautiously.

"What are you planning to do? Steal the movie? Wreck the equipment?"

Miranda hesitated. This girl could go call the cops on them. But somehow Miranda knew she wouldn't. "Both," she finally answered.

Skye nodded. "I thought so. Well, how are you going to do it?"

"What do you mean?"

"Just that. How are you going to get into the building? How are you going to shut off the alarm—because there's bound to be an alarm, if not a bunch of guards as well."

Sheepishly Miranda said, "I ... I didn't think of that. ... Um, how do you turn off an alarm?"

"You have to know the compucode."

"How do you learn that?"

"You don't."

Miranda's face fell.

"Unless ..." said Skye.

"Unless what?"

"Well, let's see. I saw something in a movie once. If you could trip the alarm and hide nearby with binoculars when the cops come to shut it off so they couldn't see you but you could watch them, then you could learn the code."

"But you'd have to be invisible to do that?"

"Exactly. That's what the character in the movie was."

Miranda frowned until she heard an "ahem" behind Skye. Slowly she looked up and met Bastable's eyes, and it was all she could do to keep from breaking into a huge grin.

Skye mistook the expression. "Look, maybe we could just write nasty slogans on the walls or something. I could help come up with some winners."

Suddenly Miranda became curious. "Why do you want to help?"

Skye answered immediately. "Because I think that Bentley Gyle person is creepy and his Hypnovision's even creepier."

"You didn't enjoy it? Even a little bit?"

"Yes, I did—and that's what really gives me the willies. To get a kick out of some device that manipulates my emotions, that makes me love and makes me hate— that's worse than creepy. That's . . . that's evil."

"Most people wouldn't agree with you," Miranda said carefully.

"Are you one of them?" Skye asked, staring directly into her eyes.

Oh, Naja, Miranda thought. *Is Skye one of us? Is she a member of the Correct Combination?* She did not really expect an answer, but she got one.

"Not member. Friend. Helpful friend," Naja said, in her mind.

Miranda took a deep breath and glanced at Bastable. He nodded agreeably. She turned back to the girl. "Skye," she asked. "How are you with surprises?"

"Try me."

"Okay," Miranda said, with another sideways look at the fenine. "We will."

CHAPTER
25

"I don't believe it," Skye said for what seemed to be the fortieth time. "What did you say you are again?"

"A fenine," Bastable told her, with, Miranda thought, an unusual display of patience.

They were no longer on the bus. The driver, annoyed by Skye's loud yelps and exclamations, had thrown them off. Now they were sitting on a bench where Skye was still trying to pull herself together. "And there's a snake in the basket," she said.

"Yes," Bastable replied. "She's a goddess. But she hasn't been well lately."

"And Chao-ji here—Iron what?"

"Dog."

"Iron Dog, he's from another world too, and Patsy . . ."

"Miranda."

". . . is from the good old U.S.A.—except over forty years ago."

"That's right."

Skye tapped both sides of her head. "If I weren't of the sanest people I know, I'd think I was going crazy. . . ." She looked at Miranda. "Tell me why you're here again."

Miranda was also being patient. She knew if she'd been in Skye's position, she probably would've acted much worse. "You were right about Hypnovision being evil,

Skye," she explained. "Everything the Charmer invents is evil, and he spreads this evil wherever he goes. We're here to defeat the Charmer, who in this place and time is a man known as Bentley Gyle. But we don't know whether or not we can because . . ."

"Because two of you are missing," Skye finished along with her. "Bennu, who's some kind of a bird, and a rat who died."

"Rattus was very brave," said Bastable quietly.

Miranda's eyes began to sting at the fenine's simple and sincere tribute. Iron Dog, who'd understood little of the conversation but all of the feelings, touched her gently on the shoulder.

Skye, drawn into the sadness, was silent until Miranda said, "You shouldn't go with us, Skye. It's dangerous, and besides . . ." You're not one of us, not one of the Correct Combination, Miranda almost said. But the persistent twinge that, even with Naja's clear acceptance, still suggested that she herself was not a proper member stopped her. ". . . and you could get hurt," she said instead. "You should go back to the Sanctuary. The trouble you're in there is nothing compared to the trouble you could be in soon."

"You don't know Ms. Saunders," Skye replied wryly, and Miranda had to smile. Then the older girl grew serious. "Look, I don't know how to put this, but, well, I told you why I left home, and what I said was true. But there was something else. Something I've never told anybody. A dream I had of a world where the Techheads rule, where nobody cares about anybody else because

they're all too busy plugged into their Telewalls and tran-
sitrons and laser swarms and stuff. In this dream, a voice
said, 'Skye, you can do something. But not now and not
alone.' Well, I've never forgotten that dream. It was . . .
it was like a glimpse of my destiny or something. I feel
that maybe I'm meeting that destiny now—and it is to
help you. Do you understand?"

Miranda paused, then said, "Yes."

"Okay. Then Bentley Gyle, look out," Skye said,
jumping up and leading them swiftly on their way.

The Hypnodrome was not the Empire State Building
or the Washington Monument, but even unlit and empty
it was obviously intended to take its place in guidebooks
as a major U.S. landmark. From the pyramidal roof to the
freestanding transparent columns beckoning one and all
to step into a new dimension, it was a site millions would
make a pilgrimage to in years to come.

"I've heard that when it's lit up the roof is iridescent
and inside the columns are holograms of historical interest created by guess who," Skye said. She shook her
head. "It's hard not to be impressed."

Miranda, and even Bastable, agreed. But Iron Dog
asked, "What is this place?" Miranda realized she had not
explained the plan to him. She did so now, telling him
how Bastable would slip in alone and trigger the alarm,
then wait until the cops arrived to learn the compucode
and deactivate the mechanism.

Iron Dog nodded and looked up at the sky. "It will be
daylight in a few hours. We must act soon."

"You're right," she agreed.

They hid across the street behind a hedge screen as Bastable, fully aware of—and only a little puffed up with—the importance of his job, entered the building. It was not long before an alarm sounded and the lights in the Hypnodrome flicked on. The noise and brightness attracted a small crowd of neighbors and passersby, none of whom noticed the tinier group who were watching the watchers.

The police arrived almost immediately and shooed the gawkers away. None of the saboteurs spoke as they waited tensely for the cops to shut off the alarm and search the building. In fact not a word was said until Bastable himself appeared shortly after the police left, startling all three humans. "Well?" Miranda asked.

"Piece of fish," the fenine replied smugly. If he'd had less furry fingers, he would've snapped them.

Skye giggled. Miranda rolled her eyes. Iron Dog scooped up Naja and the basket. Then, after checking the street for unwelcome observers, they all crossed to the Hypnodrome.

Iron Dog readied his flashlight while Bastable slipped inside the door to unlock it. "Should we split up—like we did in Rattus's laboratory?" the fenine asked as they stood in the curtained corridor.

"No," answered Miranda. "This place isn't as big and the projection room, or whatever it's called now. . . ."

"Control room," Skye put in.

"Control room," Miranda acknowledged. "It should be at the back of the auditorium, right?"

"Right," Skye agreed.

The auditorium was easy to find and its doors weren't locked. They marched quickly and easily up the aisle, past rows of plush purple cubicles, each enclosed on three sides, and climbed a short flight of steps to the control room. It was a small space lined with the most sophisticated equipment imaginable. The only simple-looking thing in the room was a trim, square box sitting on a table. The box had a slot on one side, but was otherwise tightly sealed.

"Where's the projector?" Miranda asked, puzzled.

"That's it," said Skye. "But it's called a generator."

"What? What kind of film goes in that?"

"Film? Film went out with the twentieth century. Everything's on disc now," said Skye. "Like this." She held up a thin, shiny plastic sleeve and extracted from it a thinner, shinier object.

Miranda took it and by Iron Dog's flashlight read the label. *"Mindspin."* She breathed in sharply. "This is it."

"Wow." Skye grinned at her. "This is almost too easy."

"Yes," agreed Miranda, and a tiny tremor went through her. But she chose to ignore it. There was still work to be done, and it might not prove as simple. "This generator, how can we dismantle it?" she asked.

"Well," said Skye. "We have to open it first."

"How do we do that?"

"I don't know."

They ran their hands over the top and sides but found no button, catch, or lever. They tried to lift it to check the bottom, but they could not budge it.

"Maybe we should just settle for taking the disc," Skye suggested.

But Miranda did not want to give up. Then Iron Dog casually ran his hand under the table. There was a faint *zizz* and the top of the generator opened, revealing an intricate mass of circuitry. The three humans tried to pry it loose, but it was Bastable whose sharp claws finally broke off two sequinlike chips. "Will that do the trick?" he asked.

"It'll do something," answered Skye.

"Good, then let's depart."

"Where?" Miranda asked. "Where do we go now?"

"Beach," Naja spoke, startling them. "Must go to the beach."

"Was that the snake?" Skye asked, eyes wide.

"Yes—and she's not making sense. We can't go back to the beach. We left it because of the police roundup."

"The cops will be finished by now," said Skye. "And it'll be real quiet. The beach is a good idea. We can bury this thing in the sand."

"All right," Miranda conceded, slipping the disc under her sweater. She still felt uneasy, and hoped the sensation would pass the more distance she put between herself and the Hypnodrome.

But it didn't. Throughout the bus ride, the walk to the pier, the burying of the disc, the subsequent settling down in their old places in the sand, the uneasiness prickled her, like a scratchy label in a shirt, until at last she gave up on the idea of trying to sleep and decided to take a walk alone on the beach.

It was dawn and the place was almost totally deserted; the morning sun-lovers and surfers would not arrive for at least another hour or two. But a party of young men celebrating spring break from university were sprawled on the sand, winding down from a long night of carousing. One had a blaring radio he was trying to turn down, but he was too wasted to reach the dial.

As Miranda walked by him, a voice interrupted the music pouring out of the box. "Hey, Hypnomaniacs, have we got news for you. WILD has just learned that the cops are out looking for three blutos who broke into the Hypnodrome a few hours ago, junked the generator, and bagged out with *Mindspin*. Reliable peepers have given the following description of the blutes, seen footing it from the spot: one yango, fourteen–fifteen years old, above average height, strong build, shoulder-length black hair, possibly Asian; two yinnies, one sixteen–seventeen years old, medium height, dark complexion, long hair in a braid, blue eyes; the other, twelve–thirteen, Caucasian, average height, light brown hair, has with her a round basket thought to contain the disc. Anyone spotting these scumjorks is asked to call the copshop immediately."

Mouth open, heart pounding, Miranda stood frozen, stunned by what she'd just heard. *Us. The cops are looking for us. Someone saw us and now the cops are hunting us down. But who? Who could have seen us? There was nobody. Nobody. We were careful. So careful. It was so easy. Too easy.*

Suddenly, Miranda's breath shot out of her as though she'd been struck in the stomach. He *knew. Bentley Gyle. The Charmer. When did he find out? When we got to the Hyp-*

nodrome? When we arrived in Los Angeles? Or even before? We've played right into his hands, Miranda thought. *He got rid of Rattus and Bennu, and now he'll get rid of the rest of the Correct Combination. And he won't even have to lift a finger to do it. He's got the whole Los Angeles Police Department to do it for him.*

In a panic, Miranda ran down the beach toward her friends. Maybe they could escape, maybe they could get out of the city, the state, the country even, before it was too late. They still had the basket. Maybe Naja could manage to fly it once again.

But the snake refused even to try. "We've got to leave here, Naja," Miranda pleaded. Her friends, still drowsy, huddled around. "They'll catch us. They'll put us away. Face it, Naja, the Charmer is stronger than we are. Stronger than everyone. We can't destroy him. But he can—and will—destroy us. So, please, Naja, please get us out of here."

"Can't leave. Reunion. Beach," the cobra rasped.

"Naja, listen to me. Stop saying that and listen to me. We must . . . What are you doing? Naja, where are you going?" Miranda demanded as the serpent slithered out of the basket and began to head out from under the pier onto the beach.

"Stop it. You can't go out there. What's wrong with you?" Miranda tried to pick her up, but Naja slipped out of her grasp and kept moving with incredible swiftness along the sand.

"Beach. Reunion. Beach. Reunion. Beach," she chanted, her voice growing more and more urgent.

Miranda raced after her, begging her to stay. But Naja went on until she was nearly at the water's edge. Then at last she halted and rose, hood flared, staring out at the horizon.

Miranda swore at the lightening sky and then at the snake. "Stupid. You're stupid. I'm stupid. We're all stupid. You said we could defeat the Charmer. But we can't. Your land, mine, Iron Dog's, Rattus's, Bastable's, they're all doomed. We're doomed. And Skye too. Do you hear that, Naja? Do . . ."

Suddenly, the snake quivered all over. "Reunion!" she called out, clearly, forcefully, as she stared at the sky over the sea. "Reunion. Look."

Miranda looked. At first she saw nothing but a small black dot. But it grew larger and larger, soaring nearer and nearer on its huge, many-colored wings. Miranda gave a shout of joy and amazement. It was Bennu, and in her beak wriggled Rattus, yelling, "Watch how you land, bird. I'd like to stay alive—this time."

CHAPTER
26

"Rattus. Oh, Rattus." Happy tears trickled down Miranda's cheeks as she sat on the sand hugging the rat against her. "You're all right. You're really all right, aren't you?"

"Well, yes—except for a recently developed fear of heights," he replied, looking up at the sky.

Miranda laughed. How she'd missed the rodent's wry wit, as much as his common sense.

Near them, Bastable was trying to maintain his kingly reserve, and not succeeding. "I have seen many sights in my life, but never this. Never one dead reborn," he said, his voice quavering a bit. "You . . . you were dead, were you not?"

"As a doornail," Rattus replied cheerfully. "Whatever that is."

"Then how . . . how have you come back to life?"

It was Iron Dog who answered. "Bennu," he said, his head bowed reverently to the calm, silent creature who stood by them on the sand. "She has the power to restore life."

Miranda turned to him. "Did you know all along she would restore Rattus?" she asked, confused.

"No. She cannot and will not restore all. I prayed she might help him, but I did not know—and I did not want to offer false hope."

Even false hope would have been better than no hope,

thought Miranda, but she didn't say anything. She knew
Iron Dog had meant no harm by concealing his knowledge, and besides she did not want to spoil the rejoicing.
They were together at last—all of them. The Correct
Combination in its entirety. The momentousness of that
had not yet hit her—she was still thinking only of Rattus,
alive and well.

But Skye was deeply affected by the confluence. She
stood there, a little apart from the others, awed by the
incredible sight. If meeting Bastable and hearing Naja had
tilted her world, seeing the whole Correct Combination
had turned it upside down. Despite her dream, she'd
never been a person who believed in magic—but she believed in it now, with all her heart.

"So, is this our latest addition?" Rattus said, noticing
her. "Come here. Don't be shy. Miranda will tell you my
squeak is worse than my bite."

Skye edged closer and petted the rat. "She's a friend,"
Miranda explained. "She helped stop the Charmer. Except
we haven't stopped him. He's going to stop us unless we
find someplace to hide."

"Or," added Bastable, "unless we destroy him now,
once and for all. The Correct Combination can defeat the
Charmer. Well, the Correct Combination is here. Now
Naja must tell us what to do."

They all looked at the snake who was coiled on the
sand. Miranda had thought the cobra had recovered, but
it was obvious from her glazed eyes, lackluster scales, and
dull jewel that this was not so.

"What's wrong with her?" asked Rattus.

"We don't know. She's been this way since we left Iron Dog's land. We don't know how to help her."

"Bennu does," Iron Dog spoke, daring at last to meet the benave's eyes. "Don't you?"

The benave did not answer, but ambled over to Naja with a shambling gait. Leaning down, she blinked once, twice, until a single silver drop fell from each of her eyes right onto the serpent's jewel. Then the bird straightened and waited.

Naja uncoiled slowly, forming a circle on the sand. First, she turned once clockwise, next counterclockwise, then clockwise again, and at last lay still. But only momentarily. With a faint ripping sound, her skin split neatly from her head to her tail, and a few seconds later, the snake emerged, brilliant and alert, her jewel glowing as bright as a morning star.

"Welcome back," Rattus greeted.

"The same to you," Naja replied, with a warmth in her voice that had not been there before. She looked around at the pleased but tense faces and knew what they were asking. "I must go into full shukor," she told them. "It will take time. We must hide. It is not safe here."

"But where? Where can we go?" asked Miranda. "The Sanctuary?" She looked at Skye.

The girl shook her head. "Ms. Saunders is good and kind. But she would not understand this."

"Under the pier?" suggested Bastable.

"No. The police will search there for sure," Miranda said.

"I know a place," Iron Dog spoke. "The restaurant where I worked—there is a hatch that leads to a spacious cellar with many boxes to hide behind. The lock on it was broken yesterday, and I would bet Mr. Mendez has not yet repaired it. The place itself does not open until the late afternoon, so we will be left alone there."

"Good," said Miranda, nervously glancing at the sky. "Let's go now." She hurriedly translated Iron Dog's words to Skye, helped Naja fasten herself around her waist, and reached out for Rattus.

"Just a moment," he said. "I'm partial to cellars—especially in restaurants. So I agree the place sounds great. I take it you three look normal around here. Bastable, of course, can't be seen, and Naja and I will hitch our usual ride. But what about Bennu? She's pretty conspicuous."

Iron Dog took off the cloak he'd wrapped around himself to ward off the morning chill. "If you will permit me?" he said to the benave.

Silently the bird stepped toward him. He held out the cloak to enfold her. But suddenly, she fluttered away with a shrill cry, which was immediately echoed by the shriller scream of sirens.

Iron Dog dropped the cloak, not heeding where it fell, and everyone whirled around to see half a dozen police cars barrel down over the sand and stop. Their doors flew open and twice as many cops flew out of them with their guns drawn. "Nobody move and no one will get hurt," one of them yelled through a small bullhorn.

Miranda let out a terrified, high-pitched laugh. "Do they still use bullets nowadays?" she rasped.

"I'm afraid so," was Skye's equally frightened reply.

Bastable helped Rattus quickly into the basket before the police saw the rodent. But the fenine could not figure out what else to do. There were too many people for him to attack, and he feared that any attack would set the police to firing their guns. So he stayed still.

The cops moved in two lines toward the group, preparing to cordon them off in a circle. "Put your hands slowly on top of your heads," the cop with the bullhorn told them.

Miranda and Skye obeyed at once. But Iron Dog did not understand and appealed to Miranda to explain.

"I said don't move," the cop insisted. Miranda saw his underlings' fingers twitching on their triggers.

"Don't shoot!" she begged and hurriedly told the boy what to do.

The cops drew nearer, three of them lowering their weapons to pull out handcuffs instead—thin neon-green things that Miranda guessed were probably even stronger than the old metal kind. As one approached her, she felt herself tense to meet the restraints.

But the bands never closed on her wrists, for just then there came a loud flapping, like sheets snapping in a gale. A black-draped form rose from the sand three feet into the air.

"What the hell is that?" several policemen shouted.

Another two fired their guns. But the bullets bounced harmlessly off the bucking, jouncing figure. With one tremendous lurch, it flung off its shroud, revealing itself as Bennu. Her wings now unencumbered, she began to beat them as rapidly as a hummingbird. But instead of a delicate hum, the benave's great pinions whirred like a helicopter's propellers. They stirred up the sand on the beach, whipping it, funneling it into a cyclone. It bore down on the policemen, blinding them, forcing them to their hands and knees.

Though Miranda, Iron Dog, and Skye were not in the sandstorm's direct path, they too were buffeted by it. Miranda shouted, "The basket!" and stooped down. But a gust pushed it out of reach.

"I have it!" Bastable yelled back.

"Take my hand, Miranda. You too, Bastable," Iron Dog bellowed.

"Skye, grab mine!" Miranda cried, her eyes shut against the sand. "Skye!"

"Here I am," the girl answered. Her fingertips grazed Miranda's. Then they were wrenched away. "Let me go! Let me go!"

"Skye!" Miranda screamed as the girl was pulled from her. She tried to move in her direction but found she could not. She and her friends could only move farther and farther away from Skye, from the police.

"Miranda, Iron Dog, Bastable, someone, help me! Help me!" the girl's voice, faint and disconnected, floated back.

"Skye!" Miranda wailed.

"We cannot help her," Naja's voice said in her head. "Not now. We must flee while we can."

"Skye!" Miranda cried again. But the wind swallowed the word.

"Come, Miranda," Iron Dog shouted, tugging at her until she had to follow, and taking Bastable, Naja, and Rattus with him.

A moment later, Bennu had joined them, and as one, the Correct Combination fled up the beach, leaving their friend behind.

CHAPTER
27

"Mumzum." The strange, compelling sound thrummed through the firebrick walls of the empty room that had once housed a boiler. "Mumzum." It was the third hour of Naja's shukor, and with each passing minute the tensions in the clean but cluttered cellar outside grew greater. Only Bennu, immobile on a stack of boxes, seemed calm. But no one could tell what the benave was really thinking, and the creature did not choose to share her thoughts.

In fact, no one was sharing his or her thoughts. Iron Dog did not speak of his fears for Ten-ree and his friends at home. Rattus said nothing of the odd sensation he'd had when his soul left and then returned to his body. Bastable told no tales of Appledura. And only in her head did Miranda pray for Skye. There was just one way to help her now, Miranda knew, and she waited anxiously, along with her companions, for Naja to tell her what it was.

"Mumzum!" the snake hummed, louder than ever. A pinkish light seeped through the bricks into the larger room where the others were waiting.

Hurry, Naja, Miranda urged silently—and futilely. She understood well enough that the cobra could not rush her trance. She began to pace the basement as if her walking would speed things along.

Iron Dog could not bear Miranda's pacing. It was worse than the silly figures she'd been drawing a while before on the cellar's white walls with a pencil stub she'd found on the floor. On her fifth turn, he rose and stood in front of her, put his hands on her shoulders, and gazed down until she let out a shuddering sigh and allowed him to lead her back to a spot on the floor. Then, as Ten-ree had done to him when he craved the ah-sha so badly he thought he would tear off his own skin, Iron Dog began to massage her hands, starting with the left pinky, working finger by finger, palm and palm, ending with the right one. Miranda let the soothing energy he released flow through her and out into the room. Bastable and Rattus and perhaps Bennu too seemed to feel it, and they all gathered close, absorbing one another's quiet strength.

Into that brief, serene solidarity, Naja's voice resounded, "Mumzum!" and the door of the little room flew open, smashing against the wall.

Everyone jumped. The stack of boxes Miranda and Iron Dog were leaning against tumbled down, one narrowly missing Rattus.

"Should we go in there?" the rodent asked. "See if she's all right?"

But there was no need, for the serpent herself was crawling out of the room.

They all stood up when they saw her, expectation in their eyes. She rose slowly, undulating slightly from the effects of the trance, and, saying nothing, she looked at each eager face in turn. When she met Bennu's, the benave opened her beak and sang three descending notes, then punctuated them with two rising ones, like a question mark.

"Yes, it is all clear now," Naja answered. "I have been shown how the Correct Combination can defeat the Charmer." She was silent again until Bastable could stand it no longer.

"Then tell us so that I may rid Appledura of Snare," he demanded.

"And I can say good riddance to Professor N-Chant," said Rattus.

"And to Dee Lu Shen," added Iron Dog.

"And Bentley Gyle." Miranda completed the list.

Naja raised her hood regally. Her ruby red jewel burned like fire. "For the Correct Combination to win, six must become one."

"Oh, that's really clear," Rattus grumbled.

But Iron Dog asked, "What does that mean, Naja? Do you know?"

"Yes. We must create a Sembeler—an entity that each of us must endow with one trait from himself or herself."

"An entity?" said Bastable. "How are we supposed to create an entity? In Appledura it takes five moon spans alone to bear a baby fenine, and I believe for humans here on Earth it is even longer. . . ."

"It will not take us so long with Bennu's help—for she and she alone can breathe life into the inanimate." Naja looked at the benave, who piped one note in reply.

"What do we use for the inanimate?" Rattus asked, intrigued and excited. "Does it have to have been alive?

There's a really dead mouse behind the boxes. But I think something bigger would work better."

"Something bigger would be better, and no, it does not have to have been alive. A picture will do. A drawing, even a simple one."

"Like one of these?" Rattus was examining Miranda's large and childish stick figures on the walls.

Naja turned. "Yes. One of those will do."

Miranda, who had been listening with hope and disbelief to the discussion, said, "What? You're going to use one of my doodles to defeat the Charmer?"

"No. *We* are going to use it—together. Each of us must focus on the figure and think of the gift he or she will bestow upon it—the trait that will serve the Sembeler best to defeat the Charmer."

The Correct Combination drew near the figure, Miranda last and most reluctantly, each member lightly touching those at his or her sides. "I will give the word when to speak," Naja instructed. "Now, concentrate. . . ."

Standing between Iron Dog and Bennu, Miranda closed her eyes and tried to do as the cobra told her. But she could think of nothing—no asset she had that she could give, no belief that, even with Bennu's proven talent for resurrecting the dead, the benave could bring to life this ridiculous, two-dimensional scrawl Miranda had made. The more she tried to force belief, the less she succeeded. She could sense that Iron Dog shared some of her wariness, but that he had great faith in Bennu's powers, which was sustaining him now.

After what seemed to Miranda a very long time, Naja

broke the silence. "Sembeler, hear us," she called softly. "The Correct Combination gives to you six gifts. I, Naja, the Ever-Changing, will bestow the first. I give to you the gift of vision—what others call second sight—to see into the future, to see through illusion. Take it, Sembeler, and use it well."

It was Bastable who spoke next. "Sembeler, I, Bastable the Fourth, King of the Fenines, can offer you many things—bravery, leadership, skill with a sword, a shield, a skalarac. But I think you will need most the power to make yourself invisible, and that is what I give to you. Okay, Rattus. Your turn." He nudged the rodent, who clucked his tongue but did not otherwise retort.

"Ever since I was born my mother told me, 'Rattus, if there's one thing you've inherited from your father, it's his good looks, and if there's one thing you've gotten from me, it's common sense. Since I don't think you'd find good looks much use in defeating the Charmer, I'll pass along the common sense."

Smiling despite the seriousness of the occasion, Iron Dog reached out his large hands and placed them over the figures. "I, Chao-ji, give you strength and perseverance," he said simply. Then he glanced at Miranda.

She, however, was not looking at him. She was not looking at anyone. Shame-faced, she stared down at her feet. "I . . . I have never known whether or not I was truly a member of the Correct Combination. For a while I thought perhaps I was, but now it looks as if I'm n-not, after all," she stammered. "I . . . I don't have anything to offer."

"That's not true, Miranda," Iron Dog said gently.

"You have a lot to offer," Bastable seconded.

"Yes, you do," Rattus agreed.

Miranda's head lifted a little. "What? What do I have? What gift can I bestow?"

"The most important one of all," said Naja.

Miranda's head came all the way up. "What is that?" she asked.

"Imagination," the snake replied, meeting her eyes.

Miranda blinked. A myriad of voices filled her head. "You're so imaginative." "Stop daydreaming, Miranda." "That's fantasy, Miranda. This is reality." Then her own voice, "This isn't what I imagined. This isn't like my dreams." And suddenly, though she didn't know why or how, she felt she was standing outside herself, looking at this person she'd never understood before, and she liked her. "Yes," she said. "I can offer that."

Then Bennu trundled up to the figure. She sang a brief snatch of a song, put her beak against its crude mouth, and began to blow, hard and harder still. And as the benave's breath, sweet and strong, flowed into the drawing, it filled and rounded, taking a shape that was part human, part fenine, part rodent, part snake, with here and there a touch of feathers, radiant even in the dim cellar light. When the Sembeler could grow no more, it stepped from the basement wall and stared solemnly at its creators.

"I don't believe it," Rattus cried.

But Miranda whispered, "I do."

"Is it immortal, like Bennu?" asked Bastable.

"No, Bennu can give life, but not immortality," Iron Dog said.

"Well, no matter. The Charmer doesn't have a chance now," the fenine declared.

"The Charmer always has a chance," said Naja.

Above them they heard footsteps. The restaurant was open for the day.

"It's time to leave," Miranda said. She opened the basket.

"Yes," Naja agreed.

They heard the door open. Someone was coming down the steps.

"Quickly," said Rattus.

And quickly they went, the Sembeler leading the way. Only Iron Dog, the last one into the basket, caught the startled expression of his former employer, staring not at his dishwasher, but at the new and strangely shaped hole in his cellar wall.

CHAPTER
28

Two thousand, six hundred, eighty-four hands pounded on purple canopies; two thousand, six hundred, eighty-four feet tatooed the trilonium floor. The huzzahs from one thousand, three hundred, forty-two throats, muffled by the cubicles' velvet walls, were still loud enough to make the reporters standing in the street tear their micromits from their ears in pain before they announced to the millions of eager Telewall viewers what the ecstatic audience inside the Hypnodrome had just learned—that the generator was fixed, the new disc located, and the evening's gala premiere of *Mindspin* was going to take place after all.

As if things were not clamorous enough, the decibel level rose a notch higher when the debonair man in the mylar tuxedo, who had just pumped his fist in the air in a less than debonair fashion after giving the crowd the happy news, brought onto the stage the man of the hour. Bentley Gyle did not raise his hands or voice to still the audience. He merely scanned it slowly, his eyes narrowed and focused like twin green spotlights, and everyone instantly fell silent. With cool triumph, the man let the silence stretch into a full minute before he said in a low, measured voice that nonetheless managed to reach back to the last row, "I present to you this evening the culmination of seven years of labor and devotion, a work

considered by some of the frightened and unenlightened to be so stimulating they have tried in various ways to prevent its being shown."

An angry murmur rippled through the crowd. But Bentley Gyle's eyes quieted it once again. "However, you and I know that nothing can stop progress. Nothing can halt the future. And the future is what I give you tonight." The audience began to cheer again, the noise swelling and swelling to a roof-raising pitch. Yet over it Bentley Gyle's voice effortlessly soared. "And now, brave adventurers, keep your seat belts fastened, your eyes on the screen, and let your mind spin. . . ." With an understated yet dramatic flourish, the man turned and gestured at the expansive white wall behind him.

But before the houselights had time to dim fully, through the screen's center burst a small brown missile that paused in a brief and impossible hover and then landed with hardly a bump in the dead center of the stage. The tuxedoed man ducked. The dazzled audience, seemingly oblivious to the gaping hole in the screen, continued its thunderous ovation. But Bentley Gyle dropped his hand and smiled, fiercely, viciously. "So," he hissed. "At last."

Inside the basket, the entire Correct Combination heard the words and took them for the battle cry they were. One by one they rose from the basket and confronted the man—Naja, her red jewel blazing at the green eyes; Bennu, with gleaming, hooked beak and outspread fighter-pilot wings; Bastable, whose deep growl, amplified by the stupendous sound system, rumbled like an earthquake in the audience's ears; Rattus, teeth bared and freshly sharpened; Iron Dog, unflinching and determined as a hero in an action movie; and Miranda, trying to appear as fearless and fearsome as the rest, but sensing she was not quite succeeding.

Bentley Gyle gazed back at each face, and his smile did not waver until his eyes alit on the Sembeler. Then his face paled and his emerald eyes faded briefly to aquamarine. But he gave a loud and crowing laugh, and a cold wind sprang from his lips and swept through the auditorium. The confused audience began to shiver and whimper.

"You came to see a show," the Charmer hurled at them without looking away from the Sembeler. "Well, so you shall." He snapped his fingers. The room was plunged into darkness, except for the screen which glowed a dull white. Then an image flickered onto it, flickered and steadied. It was a mountain. Silver Mountain, Miranda recognized. So did Iron Dog. He murmured the name aloud, and the words were scarcely out of his mouth when they were there.

On the pinnacle they stood, the entire Correct Combination. They could all see on the rock face below the Sembeler climbing, climbing toward a crumbling promontory on which stood a solitary man. The man turned his ravaged face toward them and yelled, "Help me!"

"Ten-ree!" Iron Dog cried, trying to go to his friend. But he could not move. None of the Correct Combination could. Only the Sembeler had the use of its arms and

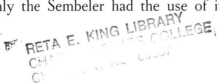

legs. Like managers at a boxing match, the Correct Combination could watch and speak, cajole or coach by words and thoughts alone.

"Where is the Charmer?" asked Bastable.

"He's got to be around somewhere," Rattus said.

Iron Dog was not listening to them. His worries were for his friend. "Sembeler, save Ten-ree!" he shouted.

The entity was too far away to hear, but it seemed to quicken its pace until it was soon pulling itself upright on the outcropping. It stretched out its hand to the outlaw.

"Yes," said Iron Dog.

"No!" warned Naja.

The boy turned his head to stare at her with anger and disbelief.

"Do not help him. Do not touch him," Naja said.

But the Sembeler had already grasped Ten-ree. And then, to everyone's horror, the outlaw writhed and twisted. His face slid away and his brown eyes flamed green until he changed into the form of Dee Lu Shen. Then he began to push the Sembeler toward the mountain's edge. They grappled ferociously. The Sembeler, with Iron Dog's gift, was strong. But the Charmer was more than his match. For every step the Sembeler thrust him away, the Charmer forced the entity back by two, until there were no more steps the Sembeler could take without tumbling into the abyss yawning just beyond its heels. The Charmer dropped his hands and grinned, playing cat and mouse with the Sembeler and the Correct Combination's hopes.

Her heart sinking, Miranda shut her eyes. But Bastable,

staring intently at the struggle, called, "Remember my gift!" The Sembeler did not seem to hear him. It raised its arms slowly to fend off the Charmer's last and fatal blow. Then it vanished.

The Charmer, momentarily startled, flailed out wildly at his foe, and something unseen struck him from behind. He grunted, trying to right himself, but instead he stumbled forward, right off the mountain. As Bastable, Rattus, and Iron Dog cheered, and Miranda opened her eyes, the Sembeler reappeared a few feet from where it had last been seen, leaning over to watch the Charmer's descent.

"The Sembeler did it!" Rattus hoorahed.

"With my help," Bastable added.

"It's over?" Miranda whispered.

No one heard her but Naja. "Not yet," the snake said, and Bennu echoed her with a harsh cry.

Then, as quick as the shift from one screen of a video game to the next, the Correct Combination found itself no longer on Silver Mountain but in Rattus's dank sewer.

Naja's jewel could not illuminate the place now, so Miranda and Iron Dog were nearly blind. But the rodent had perfect vision, and what he saw made him squeak with delight. "Buddies!" he greeted the rat army led by the old general. "Sembeler. These are my buddies."

"Your friends are here?" asked Miranda.

"Yes," Rattus answered. "And they're safe and . . ." But he didn't finish. His muzzle went stiff and his nostrils twitched. Neither Miranda nor Iron Dog nor even Bennu or Naja could tell what was making him so afraid. Only Bastable knew. He stared, awed and perplexed, as a pride of fenines, all perfect duplicates of himself, poured out of nowhere and, with green eyes gleaming bright enough to light the sewer, pounced upon the rats.

Squeals and growls and the scent of blood filled the air. Her gorge rising, Miranda had to force herself to watch. Even Iron Dog was sickened by the sight. Straining to join the fray, Rattus cursed and swore, turning his fury and anguish from the fenines before him to the one at his side. Bastable, torn by predatory desire and his attempts to restrain it, pleaded with the rat to understand and forgive. Neither of them watched the Sembeler, who jerked one way and then another, trying to decide what to do.

Its quandary caught the fenines' attention. They turned from the rats, who scuttled, limped, and crawled away into the darkness, and began to stalk the Sembeler. The entity stopped twitching and sprang to face the advancing army, all suddenly armed with swords. A sword magically appeared in the Sembeler's hand as well.

"Bastable, who are they? What are they?" Miranda cried. "They can't really be fenines, can they?"

"I don't know," said the king, shaken and ashamed, as the Sembeler's sword clashed with two others. "But there are hundreds of them, and if they fight as well as I, there's no way the Sembeler, whatever its strength, can beat them."

"Can it become invisible again?"

"Not to fenines. With them it can do nothing but fight."

And fight it did. Cutting and slashing and hacking and piercing, the Sembeler felled four fenines. Five. Six. Yet for each one it slew, two more appeared. Soon it was wounded in the shoulder, in the leg, and in the side. But still it bravely fought. Bastable, quivering and confused, shouted directions at it and at the fenines, "Retreat. Retreat. Parry. Parry. Beat. Parry. Thrust!" until he frothed at the mouth like a thing possessed.

Then Miranda gasped. A fenine's blade had stabbed the Sembeler in its sword arm, and its weapon clattered to the ground. "Oh, no! No!" Miranda cried. "Help it! We've got to help it!"

Defenseless and reeling from its wounds, the Sembeler staggered backward into a corner. The fenines grouped to deal it a mortal blow.

Then Naja rasped, "There is but one Charmer. Find him, Sembeler. See what can't be seen."

As in Iron Dog's land, the Sembeler did not turn toward the Correct Combination or appear to react. Leaning against the dripping, fetid sewer wall, it drooped and panted heavily. And the fenines pressed closer and closer, brandishing their swords.

Then the Sembeler lifted its head and gazed out at its enemies with its eyes glowing ruby red. With a swift and startling motion, it kicked its sword into its hand and plunged forward, thrusting the blade into a fenine who looked identical to the rest.

As soon as the steel entered its breast, the creature howled and the other fenines around it disappeared. With one convulsive shudder, it turned into Professor N-Chant.

"You've got me now," the little man coughed, clutching the place where his heart should have been and sinking to the ground.

Miranda's eyes opened wide. All around her the Correct Combination held their breaths as the Sembeler's sword winked out of sight and the entity stood over the fallen Charmer, dripping blood on his white lab coat.

The Correct Combination felt their invisible bonds loosen. Still scarcely daring to breathe, they turned to one another, stretching their arms or paws to embrace. Suddenly, the Charmer rose with an ear-shattering laugh. The floor beneath them split and they all fell into blackness.

Down, down they went, six Alices in the rabbit hole. But it was not Wonderland they landed in. It was the hard obsidian floor of Naja's gorgeous temple. And the Sembeler fell with a thump into the goddess's throne, once encrusted with rubies but now with emeralds and emblazoned with the image of the new green-eyed god. Immediately, a net of green filaments spun across the entity's weary, bloodied body, imprisoning it there. With a groan it fought to gather its strength and began to strain against the web. But the more it pushed, the tighter the strands grew until the Sembeler had to stop before they cut into its flesh. As the Correct Combination watched it with mounting despair, a cold, disembodied voice announced, "And we condemn this place as a temple of false gods and consign it to oblivion." Then there was silence, thick as the dust that came sprinkling from the ceiling, coating the golden statues, dulling the polished floor.

Miranda felt its smothering weight upon her shoulders and was filled with a dread far worse than any she'd felt before. She knew the voice belonged to the Charmer. But where was he? Was he here, invisible, in the room? Or was his voice coming to them from somewhere else? When would he arrive? Who would he be this time? She opened her mouth to ask and Naja said, "He is not here —and he will not be."

"He won't?" said Iron Dog; "Why not?" Rattus asked; "Then he is a coward," Bastable sneered—all three at the same time.

But Miranda met Naja's eyes and knew what the snake was thinking. *He will not come because he believes there's no need. He will let us die here alone, or worse, he will let us live—talking heads trapped for all eternity in useless bodies.* She shuddered, and she felt Iron Dog and Bastable shudder too as the realization seeped into them. Only Bennu seemed unperturbed. *She's used to timeless sleep,* Miranda thought.

But the benave was not sleeping now. She was blowing her warm, fragrant breath toward the Sembeler as hard as she could. It reached the figure only as the merest wisp of air—not enough to heal its wounds, but balm enough to soothe their pain and let the Sembeler renew its struggle against its bonds. Yet still it couldn't free itself from the wicked web, and soon its strength began to ebb once more.

"You know," said Rattus with more matter-of-factness than he actually felt, "my mother always said that sometimes to retreat is the best way to go forward. It sounds stupid, but I tried it once when I was caught in a rat trap, and it works."

Though his voice was small and there was no way the Sembeler could have heard him, almost at once the entity stopped thrashing against its bond. It sat still, as if thinking. Then slowly it reached below and began to tug at the cushion on which it sat. The pad was not tightly fastened and it came away rather easily. Grunting and shifting, the Sembeler worked it free and down the undersides of its legs.

"What is it doing?" Miranda asked.

"Using common sense," said Iron Dog, shooting Rattus a grin.

With the cushion gone, the Sembeler, now several inches lower and a bit farther back on the throne, pried out a tack from the seat. Reaching awkwardly behind, it slashed the sharp point through the padded back. The brocade was thick, with sturdy metallic threads, and the Sembeler's arm was bent at a painful angle. But the entity did not give up. Again and again it ripped at the fabric until it finally made a thin gash. Next it reached inside and began to tear out handfuls of stuffing, tossing them one by one on the floor, until the pad flattened. Then the Sembeler slid backward, the web pulling away from its body, until it was pressed against the throne's stiff spine. Sucking in its belly and breath, it slipped down and out from underneath the nasty net. With renewed strength, it strode to the altar, seized a broken statue, and returned to the throne, where it smashed it against the Charmer's image. The face cracked. There was a sharp cry. And the Correct Combination found itself free.

Then the temple began to shake. A pillar buckled. A piece of ceiling collapsed. "Hurry," Naja warned. "To the stairs." She slithered away.

Bastable, Rattus, Bennu, Iron Dog, and Miranda all rushed to follow her. They reached the door. It splintered in two with a groan. They stumbled through and found themselves on the Hypnodrome's stage.

On the screen behind them, Naja's temple lay in ruins. From out of the wings Bentley Gyle appeared to a standing ovation from all the audience.

"What is this? What now?" Iron Dog asked, and Miranda heard, for the first time, true fear in his voice.

"They think we're part of the show," Rattus told him.

"And so you are," said Bentley Gyle. "So you all are. My movie. My show. You always were. You always will be."

"*I* won't, Charmer," Bastable snarled.

"Yes, you will, my dear deposed king. You have no choice. None of you has. Not the goddess here, not even the immortal."

A wave of hopelessness washed over the Correct Combination. Miranda felt herself drowning in it. *Doomed*, she heard herself say on the beach. And the word resounded in her head. *Doomed, doomed.* She clapped her hands over her ears and huddled down, moaning. Yet she could still hear the Charmer add his sour grace note.

"Your miserable puppet can't help you now," he said, pointing to the entity who lay crumpled much like a marionette on the floor. "It has used all your tokens."

Miranda blinked, her next thought coming slowly, like a fluorescent light turning on. *But that's wrong. The Charmer is wrong. The Sembeler still has my gift.*

She lowered her hands from her head and turned to

the entity. *Could it be? Could my gift help it, help us? Impossible. The Charmer has strength. The Charmer has power. He can create. He can destroy. Yet Naja said my gift was the most important of all. How? How can my imagination defeat the Charmer?*

And then the answer came, an answer so clear and perfect she could scarcely believe it was so. The Sembeler knew it too. It rose and glided to the laughing Charmer, who stopped in mid-peal. In Miranda's voice it said, "You think you have won, Charmer. You think we will be or do whatever you imagine. But my imagination is stronger. I imagine you gone—from my world and all the worlds I've seen and dreamed—now and for all time."

The Charmer began to shudder. He swung his arm at the still-roaring audience, which suddenly disappeared, then at the screen, which lit up brightly except for the dark gaping hole in its center. "You can't!" he screamed as an unseen force began to drag him toward the hole. "You can't!" he shrieked as he dug his heels into the ground, to no avail. "You can't!" he bellowed as he flew through the gap. His voice echoed briefly as the screen collapsed in on him and vanished from sight.

There was total silence then. And in it the Sembeler came to the Correct Combination and bowed to each member. Then, before Miranda had time to laugh or sigh, it faded away, leaving her and her friends alone on the empty stage.

CHAPTER
29

The celebration was a noisy one. Rattus turned circles, his squeals rebounding off the theater's bare walls. Bennu soared up into the flies, trumpeting her loud triumphal cries to the spotlights. Bastable had a rare and most undignified fit—racing up and down the boards of the stage like a common cat, dashing up the curtains and back down again. Even Naja rose and swayed back and forth to a music no one else could hear. Only Iron Dog and Miranda, sitting on the edge of the stage, their backs to the empty seats, watching the antics of their friends, were subdued.

"He's really gone, isn't he?" Miranda said quietly.

"He's gone."

"I don't believe it."

"Yes you do. If you didn't, he'd still be here."

Miranda turned and smiled shyly. "It wasn't just me. It really was all of us, the whole Correct Combination. Without everyone's gifts, we would have lost long ago."

Iron Dog smiled back, a smile that said so many things. Then his eyes shifted and he lowered them. "There will be much to do," he said, rather gruffly.

"Where?" Miranda asked.

"At home." The words dropped between them like pebbles disturbing a placid pool.

"Home," Miranda repeated with a rueful chuckle. For

a few hours, a few days even, she'd actually forgotten about home, about her parents. What were they doing now? How many days had passed for them since their daughter went away? Would they still know her? Would she still know them? There was only one way to find out, and that was to go home. Could she do that? She looked up at Naja.

The snake was no longer swaying. She was perched atop the softly glowing basket, staring at Miranda. *Yes*, said her eyes. *You can go home. But do you want to?*

Miranda glanced from the snake to the rest of her friends, now settling down, tired and content, in the center of the stage. *I'll have to say good-bye to them all. Everyone—even Bastable.* "Why can't we all stay together?" she said mournfully, not realizing she'd spoken aloud.

Everyone heard her. Feeling her sadness, they gathered near.

"Where would we stay, Miranda?" said Rattus.

"In whose world?" Bastable asked.

Mine, she wanted to say, but she knew that was not how it could be. Each of her friends would miss his or her place, his or her home. Just as she would, as she did right now.

"Let us bid our farewells now," Naja suggested, "while just the six of us are together."

"Yes," agreed Iron Dog. "While we are alone."

Then the members of the Correct Combination turned to one another to say good-bye. Bennu sang hers, a different melody for each friend. Naja nodded at each, then beamed a ray from her jewel at his or her heart. Rattus said a few flippant words to everyone. To Bastable, these were, "If you're ever near my sewer, call first before you drop in, cat."

"I'll remember that, rat," Bastable replied, and his dry tone did not entirely hide the fondness underneath.

Iron Dog's good-byes were solemn and formal until he reached Miranda, who had not been able to say good-bye to anyone without weeping. For a moment the two just gazed at one another. Then he hugged her, longer than mere friends might, but not long enough for ones who were parting forever.

When they broke apart at last, they saw that their other friends were waiting by the basket.

"We are ready now?" Naja asked.

"We are ready," said Iron Dog. One by one they climbed inside and then spun away through space and time.

They went first to Iron Dog and Bennu's homeland. Miranda saw the boy reunited safely with Ten-ree and his other friends on Silver Mountain, while the benave joined her companions and left for the forest to summon Chi-wa and Chi-na and all the other guardian spirits to help rebuild and harmonize their world.

Rattus's turn was next. The basket took him to the laboratory where Professor N-Chant's dusty, abandoned papers were being eaten by a small band of rats. To Miranda's amazement, the old general was among them, and he greeted Rattus like a long-lost relation—which, in fact, he probably was.

"Now we will take you back to your land, to your own time," Naja told Miranda as the basket took off once again.

My land. My own time, Miranda thought. *What will it be like in Skye's time now? Skye. I never got to say good-bye to her. I never found out what happened to her.*

"Would you like to see?" asked Naja, though Miranda had not spoken.

"Can I?" she asked, aloud this time.

In answer, Naja's jewel winked, and the bottom of the basket turned silver, then white, then transparent. Through it Miranda could see a street that looked familiar and a striking building with an iridescent pyramid on top that was even more so. There was a sign on the building, though Miranda could not make out the letters, and many people standing in front by its pillars, as if anticipating a grand event. "The Hypnodrome!" Miranda gasped. "The premiere, it's happening after all."

"No. It is not," said Naja. And as the basket came a bit nearer Miranda could read the sign at last. It said: "U.E.C."

"United Earth Council," explained Naja. "The first successful planetary government, dedicated to the belief that compassion must always overrule profit, that technology exists to serve people and not vice versa. This building is its new home. These delegates await the new Chief Consul."

As Miranda looked on, the delegates, of many races and nationalities, turned eagerly to watch a small, round vehicle glide up to the building. A tall woman with light brown skin and crinkly hair got out of it, flanked by another thinner woman and a plump man. To the steps they strode. There, while cameras—or what Miranda took to be cameras—rolled and people listened, the tall woman made a short speech. Then she unlocked the building's doors. The people cheered and applauded. The woman smiled at them, her smoky blue eyes shining.

"Skye!" Miranda exclaimed with delight. "It's Skye! She's the Chief Consul."

"Yes," said Naja. "And a brilliant one she will be."

"Skye," Miranda repeated, feeling happy tears form. She brushed them away. Then softly she asked, "Does she remember us, Naja? Does she remember me?"

"Yes. She remembers you, Miranda. She always will."

"Oh, I wish I could be around when she's Chief Consul. I wish I could see the way my world turns out then."

"Perhaps you will be," Naja said.

Miranda did not press her to explain further, nor did the cobra offer any more words.

Then the bottom of the basket grew dark again, and Skye and all the other people disappeared from view. Back through time the basket whirled, and faster than Miranda could say her address, she was home.

"We have said our farewells, so we need not say them again," Naja said as Miranda lifted the lid of the basket.

"Right," Bastable agreed. "Then kindly take me home. Appledura awaits my return."

"Wait, Bastable," Miranda stopped him. "We haven't said our good-byes yet."

"Oh. All right. Good-bye then," the fenine said tersely.

"Bastable!" Miranda couldn't believe his tone. "Aren't you going to miss me at all?"

"I don't plan to miss you, Miranda," was Bastable's curt reply.

So hurt she couldn't say another word, Miranda stepped out of the basket. Her feet had scarcely touched the floor when it flashed silver and disappeared. Tears running down her cheeks, she stared at the empty space where it had been. Then she glanced around her room. In the rich moonlight pouring through the open window, the place looked exactly the same—not a stick of furniture was different, not a knickknack was out of place. Blinking away the tears, she reached to turn on the light, and then she heard the key turning in the front door lock. Without pausing to think, she opened her closet door and dived in.

She heard footsteps in the hall and her door knob turning, and she smelled her mother's favorite perfume as she entered the room. Opening the door a crack, Miranda peered at her mother, who was now leaning over her bed. "Miranda? Where are you, Miranda?"

Miranda opened the closet door wider. It creaked. Her mother turned around, her gown, the same one she'd been wearing the night Miranda left, swirling out in a dark circle around her. "Miranda! What are you doing there? Why aren't you in bed?"

Awkwardly coming closer, Miranda peered at her mother's face, which the moonlight illuminated clearly. It had not aged one day. "Mom, what time is it?"

"A little after midnight."

"Oh, uh, on what day?"

"The day after the day before," her mother teased.

"What, um, year?"

"What kind of guessing game is this, Miranda? It's nineteen ninety, of course. Were you having another daydream?"

"Maybe," Miranda replied.

"Well, you should be having a *night* dream. Get into your pajamas and . . . What are you wearing? It looks like your dad's sweater."

"I was cold."

"Really? I hope you're not getting sick." She felt Miranda's forehead. "You don't feel warm. Maybe you're just sleepy. Change your clothes and get right into bed."

"Okay." Automatically, Miranda reached under her pillow. Her pajamas were there, neatly folded as always. Her mother watched as she put them on and slid under the covers. Then she bent down to kiss her.

"Did you . . . did you and Dad miss me tonight, Mom?" Miranda asked.

"Why, of course we did," was her mother's surprised reply.

But Miranda didn't believe her. After her mother left, she lay in bed in her safe, quiet room, wondering if anyone anywhere would ever miss her, and feeling lonelier than she'd ever felt. Even hanging out with Suzanne and Amy Beth and Pamela would be better than this. *Actually, that Pam really isn't so bad. Maybe I'll invite her over tomorrow,* she told herself. *Maybe I'll tell her about my adventures.* But she knew that she never would, and fat tears began to fall from her eyes again, followed by several large sobs even her pillow couldn't stifle.

"By King Mastermain," a familiar voice said, "you humans certainly do enjoy a good cry."

Miranda pulled the pillow from her face and sat up. Bastable was standing there, all by himself, at the foot of her bed.

"Bastable! Oh, Bastable, you're back!" she cried, leaping up and hugging him.

He fidgeted and squirmed, but was polite enough not to pull away or scratch her arms, until she let him go. "Well, of course I'm back. I said I didn't plan to miss you, did I not?"

Miranda laughed, louder than she'd intended, and then abruptly stopped. "But how . . . how did you get back? The basket's gone."

"I found the door between worlds. It took me seven months. . . ."

"Seven months! But you left only an hour ago."

"An hour here perhaps, seven months in Appledura. At any rate, I found it and I marked it well, so I'll always be able to find it whenever I choose."

"But that's wonderful!"

"Yes, and now it's time to go."

"Go? Go where?"

"Why, to Appledura, of course—the door's open to you too. There's a festival there in our honor that I'm certain you won't want to miss. You know the other honorees who are attending—although you may not recognize Rattus. My fenines are well-behaved, but the sight of a rat on parade may tempt even the most noble. So we devised a bit of a disguise, Naja and I—something of a cross between a lizard and a very small dog. Rattus was not entirely grateful, but that's a rodent for you. . . . Now, put on your finery, Miranda. This is a gala affair. Even Iron Dog's outfit is better than that." He touched her pajama top.

Miranda was beginning to giggle. "How about if I go in *fish*net stockings and a *herring*bone suit?" she asked.

"You're making a joke, aren't you, Miranda?"

"Yes."

"I thought so." Bastable frowned. "Except I still don't get it."

"That's okay," Miranda said, quickly slipping into her prettiest party dress and her fanciest shoes. "I'll explain it to you—on the way to Appledura." Then she held out her arm. Bastable looped his tail around her wrist, and in one moment more, they were on their way.